and the
RAIDERS of the
LOST ARK

INDIANA JONES™

and the
RAIDERS of the
LOST ARK

Ryder Windham

**Based on the story by George Lucas and Philip Kaufman
and the screenplay by Lawrence Kasdan**

LUCAS BOOKS

HarperCollins*Childrensbooks*

Indiana Jones and the Raiders of the Lost Ark
First published in Great Britain by HarperCollins Children's Books in 2008

2

978-0-00-727675-2

A CIP record for this title it available from the British Library.
No part of this publication may be reproduced, stored in a retrieval system or
transmitted in any form or by any means, electronic, mechanical, photocopying,
recording or otherwise, without the prior permission of HarperCollins Publishers Ltd,
77-85 Fulham Palace Road, Hammersmith, London, W6 8JB.
The HarperCollins Children's Books website is:
www.harpercollinschildrensbooks.co.uk
Printed and bound in Great Britain

Thanks to Annmarie Nye at Scholastic, and Jonathan Rinzler and Leland Chee at Lucasfilm. Thanks also to the authors of Lucasfilm's official *Indiana Jones* website (www.indianajones.com), and to Dr. David West Reynolds for his extensive knowledge about the costumes, props, and vehicles in the *Indiana Jones* films.

For Anne,
who knows what belongs in a museum

INDIANA JONES

and the
RAIDERS of the
LOST ARK

aking his way up along a narrow trail at the edge of the Peruvian rain forest, Indiana Jones used the back of his hand to wipe the sweat from his unshaven face. The whiskers didn't hide the thin scar that traveled across his chin, just below his lower lip — not that he cared. He'd had the scar for years, and never spent much time in front of a mirror anyway. Besides, a shaving kit would have been just one more thing to carry. As far as he knew, there wasn't any reward waiting for a man who died in the jungle with a clean shave.

Jones looked at a mountain peak in the distance to confirm he was still headed in the right direction. To protect himself from the elements, he wore a weathered felt fedora, a battered brown leather jacket, and durable high-top leatherwork boots. Under his jacket he wore a light khaki safari-style shirt. A cotton web belt held up his dark khaki pants, and a second belt, made of leather, carried his holstered revolver and coiled bullwhip. He also toted a faded green-fabric shoulder bag that contained several small provisions.

Although he looked more like a wayward cowboy than a thirty-six-year-old university professor, he was in fact a respected archaeologist who taught at Marshall College in Connecticut. His friends called him "Indy," but the seven men who followed him through the jungle were hardly his friends.

Two of the men, Satipo and Barranca, were Peruvians who wore tattered, sweat-stained jungle khakis. Indy had hired them as guides. He had met them at a remote river outpost called Machete Landing, where they had no small reputation as thieves. Unfortunately, the motley pair also had a fragment of a map and some knowledge of the route to Indy's destination, the lost temple of the Chachapoyan warriors. Indy might have eventually found the lost temple on his own, but that would have taken more time, and he was certain that at least one treasure hunter had a head start on him. Still, Indy had no reason to trust Satipo and Barranca, and knew better than to pay thieves too much money in advance.

The other five men who trailed behind Indy were indigenous Quechuans, who'd been hired on as porters for the expedition. They wore ponchos and brightly colored knitted caps, and barely made a sound as they moved through the jungle. Aided by two donkeys, the Quechuans were laden with equipment and provisions, including special tools and drinking water. The Quechuans had been reluctant to travel in Indy's group because they were afraid of the Chachapoyan temple. They believed it was cursed.

The year was 1936. A few weeks earlier, Adolf Hitler, the leader of the Nazi Party in Germany, had presided over the Games of the XI Olympiad in Berlin. Indy would always remember those games because the American track and field athlete Jesse Owens had won four gold medals. Most Peruvians were still grumbling about the notorious football tournament quarterfinals. Peru had defeated Austria 4–2 in overtime, but then withdrew in protest after Austria raised complaints about their conduct, and game officials ordered a rematch. Even Satipo and Barranca were enraged when Peru's president announced that a "crafty Berlin decision" had cost the Peru team their victory, and allowed Austria to claim the silver medal. Now, both guides hoped to console their country's loss by claiming any treasure they might find for themselves.

Indy's group proceeded deeper into the jungle. Soon, they reached an area where the donkeys could no longer maneuver between the trees, and they were forced to leave them behind. Satipo obligingly pulled on a backpack to help the porters carry provisions, but Barranca had refused to carry anything except his heavy revolver, which was already holstered at his belt.

Indy was tired. Hungry, too. But he stayed alert, keeping his eyes and ears open. He hadn't expected to hear one of the men in his party scream, but when it happened, he didn't flinch either.

The scream came from one of the Quechuan porters. While pushing away some leaves, the man had suddenly found himself staring into the glaring eyes of a massive stone face, a demon with a wide, snarling mouth. Startled birds shrieked and flew out from the undergrowth. As the panicked Quechuan ran from the monstrous statue, all the other porters followed his example and retreated swiftly into the jungle.

Indy, Satipo, and Barranca made no effort to stop the porters. Ignoring the birds that whipped around the statue, Indy pulled an aged piece of parchment from his pocket and examined it. The parchment, which he'd brought with him from the United States, was part of an old map. He hadn't told Satipo and Barranca about the parchment, but he was aware of their silence as they watched him from behind.

If this map is good, Indy thought, *there'll be a stream just east of here.* Indy looked to his left, and then moved away from the gaping statue as he tucked the map back into his pocket. Satipo and Barranca followed.

They found the stream and crossed it, and it seemed that the surrounding jungle grew even darker. A few long shafts of light, slicing down through the thick forest canopy, were the only evidence that it was still daytime. Indy lowered the brim of his hat to protect his eyes from the brilliant shafts, and searched the trees for any sign that he was still heading in the right direction.

Then he saw the dart. It was just a thin needle of wood, embedded in the otherwise smooth trunk of a tall tree. Indy stopped to pull the dart from the tree, slid his fingers over it to feel a slightly tacky substance on its tip, then dropped it and moved on.

Watching Indy's actions with curiosity, the two guides scurried over to where Indy had been standing. Satipo picked up the dart. Studying the small projectile, he said nervously, "The Hovitos are near." Satipo rubbed the dart's tip with his fingers, felt the tacky substance, and then stuck a finger in his mouth. An instant later, he spat hard. "The poison is still fresh . . . three days." He glanced back at the way they had approached the tree from the jungle. "They're following us."

Barranca snatched the dart from Satipo's hand and took a close look at it for himself. "If they knew we were here," he said, "they would've killed us already." He dropped the dart, and then both men stepped away from the tree to resume following the American professor.

Soon, the three men arrived upon a narrow river. Indy stopped and extended his open hand to Satipo. Satipo reached into a tattered pocket to remove the map fragment he had shown Indy back at Machete Landing, and handed it over to Indy. Then Indy reached into his own pocket to remove the piece of parchment that he had consulted earlier. Both Satipo and Barranca watched intently as Indy, facing the river, held the two fragments up side by side. Despite the frayed and crumpled edges, it was obvious Indy had just reunited two parts of a single map.

While Satipo watched in astonishment, Barranca silently fumed. On several occasions, the two thieves had used their partial treasure map to lure adventurers into the jungle, only to rob and kill their greedy victims. But they never knew for certain that the map was good for something beyond their scams, not until now. And the only thing stopping Barranca and Satipo from using the assembled map to find the treasure themselves was Indiana Jones.

Barranca had always been more daring and impatient than his relatively cautious partner, and he decided it was high time to kill the American. He shifted his position behind Indy, drew his own revolver from its holster, aimed it at his target's back, and thumbed back the gun's hammer.

Clack.

The mechanical sound of the gun's hammer was out of place in the jungle, and Indy's keen ears recognized it at once. His right hand dropped to the bullwhip at his belt as he spun to face Barranca. Faster than thought, the ten-foot-long whip lashed out with a deafening *CRACK*, biting into the flesh of Barranca's gun hand. The thief gasped in pain and dropped his weapon. The revolver fired as it struck a rock before it slid into the river. Staring at Indy with wide-eyed terror, Barranca clutched at his damaged wrist, then turned and ran off into the jungle.

As for Satipo, he was stunned in a different way. He could not recall Barranca ever being defeated in a fight, nor had he ever seen anyone move as fast as Indiana Jones. He knew if he fled with Barranca, he'd never see the treasure that Indy sought. Granted, he also knew that it wouldn't be easy to take that treasure away from Jones. Satipo watched without a word as the grim American recoiled his whip.

Indy sensed instinctively that Satipo was torn between fear and greed. It was only because he imagined that he might still require at least one assistant that he didn't send Satipo running, too. With some reluctance, he allowed the trembling guide to follow him away from the riverbank.

The two men turned up a muddy hill, where they found a dark, rocky outcropping covered with a thick tangle of vines. Indy pushed the vines aside to reveal the entrance to a cave.

"This is it," Indy said as he reached into Satipo's backpack and removed an empty canvas drawstring bag. Bending down, Indy filled the small bag with loose sand from outside the cave as he added, "This is where Forrestal cashed in."

"A friend of yours?" Satipo asked.

"A competitor," Indy said. As he tied off the bag of sand and tucked it into his shoulder bag, he added, "He was good. He was very, very good."

Looking from the cave's dark entrance to Indy, Satipo said, "Señor, nobody's come out of there alive!" Fearing for his own safety, Satipo added, "Please . . ."

Indy turned Satipo around to access the man's backpack. He quickly removed a long-handled torch as he pulled the pack off Satipo, and then tossed the pack to the ground. He lit the torch, handed it to Satipo, and led the nervous thief into the cave.

Thick veils of spiderwebs stretched across the opening, and Indy pushed them aside with his coiled whip. Moving slowly and carefully, the two men made their way up an inclined passage. Soon, it opened into a larger chamber, where plant life and stalactites hung from the damp ceiling. The place was filled with the smell of jungle rot, and the echoing sounds of dripping water and skittering creatures. As Indy advanced across the chamber floor, Satipo's hoarse voice croaked from behind. "Señor —"

Indy halted and turned slowly to face Satipo, who was trying not to tremble as he held the torch. Satipo was staring at the back of Indy's leather jacket. Indy craned his neck to see three large black tarantulas crawling up his back. Once again utilizing his rolled whip, he reached back casually to brush off the tarantulas, letting them fall to the ground.

Then Satipo's eyes went wide as he noticed a tarantula moving on his own right shoulder. He was too scared to speak, but Indy heard the man gasp and saw what he was looking at. Indy raised a hand and made a spinning motion with his fingers, gesturing for Satipo to turn around slowly. Satipo obeyed, and turned to reveal that his back was covered by at least two dozen tarantulas. Tightening his grip on the lower neck of the blazing torch, Satipo audibly gulped for air while Indy flicked off the tarantulas and let them scuttle away into the darkness.

Satipo was still breathless as he followed Indy deeper into the cave. He nearly jumped out of his skin when Indy broke the silence with a single word: "Stop." Indy had noticed a shaft of bright sunlight that angled down through the ceiling and interrupted their path up ahead.

Indy didn't know just how deep underground they were, but given that there wasn't any rubble on the ground beneath the light shaft, he was pretty sure that the sunlight hadn't entered by way of a random cave-in. *Might be a trap*, he thought. Glancing back at Satipo, Indy cautioned, "Stay out of the light."

While Satipo cowered and clung to the shadows against the cave's dirt wall, Indy ducked under the light shaft and moved a few feet forward. Standing just to the side of the light shaft, Indy raised his left hand into the light and felt the briefest moment of warmth against his skin, then dropped his arm fast.

There was a loud *whoosh* as a row of long, sharp spikes sprung out from the sides of the chamber, spearing the area below the light shaft. Satipo screamed, not because he had been wounded, but because there was a dead man's impaled body embedded on the spikes. Clad in a khaki safari shirt similar to Indy's, the corpse trembled as the trap's sudden, forceful motion came to an abrupt stop. Satipo screamed louder as the corpse's head involuntarily twisted to face Indy. Even though half of

the man's face was gone, Indy recognized what was left.

"Forrestal," Indy muttered. It didn't give him any pleasure to see how his former competitor had met his end. Giving the corpse a last look, Indy thought, *You should have stayed home.*

After Satipo recovered his nerve, he followed Indy into the next passage, where they were pleased to find that there was enough natural light coming down through the open ceiling that they no longer required the torch. Unfortunately, they found their path interrupted again, this time by a deep, open pit with steep, vertical walls. Standing at the edge of the pit, Indy gauged the distance across the pit to be about twelve feet. Indy knew his limitations and decided to leave the long jumps to Jesse Owens.

Indy looked at the ceiling above the pit and spotted an exposed wooden beam, then swung his whip. It wrapped tightly around the beam, and Indy tugged at the whip's handle to make sure the beam would hold his weight. Keeping his grip tight on the handle, he leaped out and swung over the pit to land on the far side of the passage. Then he threw the handle of the whip back to Satipo, who caught it and repeated Indy's action. But as Satipo swung out over the pit, the beam above his head suddenly shifted, just as his feet touched down beside Indy.

Holding tight to the whip, Satipo cried out as he lost his balance and began to fall backwards into the pit. Indy lunged forward and grabbed Satipo's belt, then hauled him up to safety. Satipo threw his arms around his rescuer so tightly that Indy could feel the frightened man's heart pounding against his chest.

Indy moved Satipo away from the edge of the pit, then — leaving the whip's tip curled around the upper beam — he wedged the whip's handle between some vines that traveled up the walls. Indy didn't want to proceed without his whip, but if they had to exit the temple in a hurry, they'd have to cross that pit again. It just seemed smart to leave it there.

Indy and Satipo exited the passage and rounded a corner to find themselves in another chamber. It was a large domed room with a stone floor in an intricate design. Passing a huge brass sun against a nearby wall, Indy realized they had reached the temple's sanctuary. But the brass sun held little interest for Indy and Satipo, for both men had their eyes trained on the far side of the chamber. There, at the top of a short flight of stone steps, a cylindrical stone table stood in the middle of what appeared to be an altar. And on top of that table, resting on a circular stone pedestal just a few inches high, was a gold figurine about the size of a human skull.

Indy had come a long way from Connecticut in search of the Golden Chachapoyan idol. At last, there it was, right in front of him.

But it wasn't in his hands yet.

CHAPTER TWO

atipo glanced at Indy, and knew at once that the gold idol was his objective. Eager to leave the temple, Satipo said, "Let us hurry. There is nothing to fear here."

Satipo began to walk fast in the direction of the idol, but Indy caught him by the shirt and practically slammed him against the wall. All it took was one wrong move to wind up like Forrestal. *Nothing to fear?* Keeping his grip on Satipo, Indy looked again at the wide-open path to the idol and said, "That's what scares me."

Indy released Satipo, and then reached for an old, unlit wooden torch that hung against the wall. Taking the torch, Indy squatted down to examine a dirt-caked stone tile on the floor. He held the torch upright over the tile and used its tip to gently push away the grime, revealing a narrow gap around the edges of the tile. *Another trap*, Indy thought.

He brought the torch down upon the tile to find out what would happen if a man were to step on it. The tile sank slightly into the floor and a tiny arrow suddenly launched out from the wall, slamming into the torch. Satipo blinked in surprise. Indy followed the arrow's trajectory and saw that it had been blown out through the mouth of one of the carved masks that decorated the altar's walls. It was a nasty but effective security system.

Indy handed the torch to Satipo, then rose and said, "Stay here."

"If you insist, señor," Satipo said with a self-satisfied smile. He was happy to let Indy do all the work.

Indy rubbed his fingers together as he gazed at the idol on the far side of the altar. It looked so easy. All he had to do was walk across the chamber, climb the steps, grab the idol, and walk back the same way. The only hitch was that there were a lot of stone tiles between him and the idol, and the walls were lined with numerous stone masks, all of which had dark holes for eyes and mouths. One wrong step and Indy would be a human pincushion.

Indy made a quick study of the tiles, noting the ones that had loose dirt around them or appeared to protrude from the floor more than others, and took a cautious step forward. Then another — and another. On either side of him, the stone masks stared at him with their deadly, hollow eyes. He risked a glance forward to the gold idol, which had a snarling face and angry eyes. If Indy had been a superstitious man, he might have suspected that the idol was watching him, cursing his every step.

Indy nearly lost his balance, and he heard Satipo gasp behind him as he jumped up the stone steps, doing his best to keep his boots on the tiles that looked safe. He continued forward until he stood before the altar, then he slowly crouched down so his eyes were level with the idol's.

Indy stroked his bristly chin as he contemplated the idol and the circular stone pedestal upon which it rested. Because the temple's builders booby-trapped the floor, he figured the idol would be similarly rigged. Fortunately, Indy had come prepared.

He reached for the bag of sand that he'd collected from outside the cave. Examining the statue, he guessed that its weight was slightly less than the bag. He removed some sand, letting it slip through his fingers onto the floor beside the table, then clutched the bag in his right hand to one side of the idol while positioning his empty left hand on the idol's other side. He held his breath.

In a swift, fluid motion, Indy used his left hand to pluck the idol from its pedestal in the same split second that he rolled the sand-filled bag onto the pedestal. Then

Indy froze, waiting for something to happen, but nothing did.

Indy looked at the idol in his hands, exhaled, and then grinned. *It worked!* But as he began to turn away from the table, he heard a grinding sound, and glanced back to see the pedestal descending into the center of the table.

Uh-oh.

There came a low rumble all around the altar, and then thick streams of dust and heavy stones began crashing down from the ceiling. Disregarding the rigged tiles on the floor, Indy bolted away from the table and leaped down the stone steps. Behind him, a hail of small arrows launched from the hollows of the carved masks on the surrounding walls. Indy lowered his head and kept running and felt several arrows skim the back of his jacket.

Satipo had already started running from the crumbling sanctuary, and he arrived in the passage with the deep pit before Indy did. When Indy rounded the corner to enter the passage, he saw that Satipo had used the stashed whip to swing back to the other side of the pit. Satipo held the whip by its handle, but the whip's other end was no longer wrapped around the beam, which appeared to have been further dislodged from the ceiling.

"Give me the whip!" Indy shouted.

Keeping his grip on the whip, Satipo shouted back, "Throw me the idol!" From behind Satipo, there came yet another grinding sound as an ancient mechanism began to slowly lower a wide, heavy stone to block the only exit from the passage. "No time to argue!" Satipo said as he glanced from the descending stone to Indy. "Throw me the idol, I throw you the whip!"

Without much of a choice, Indy tossed the idol over and across the pit. Satipo caught it. Then Indy shouted again, "Give me the whip!"

Satipo grinned deviously as he dropped the whip, letting it fall to the ground at his feet. "Adiós, señor," he said, before he turned and ducked under the still-descending slab of rock to escape.

Earlier thoughts of Olympic broad jumps had left Indy's mind. His only thought was to stay alive and — if possible — get the idol back from Satipo. He took three running steps forward, and then sprang over the pit.

He almost made it. He caught the pit's opposite edge with his stomach and elbows. Ignoring the pain, he dug his fingertips into the loose dirt, struggling for leverage as his boots kicked at the walls below. Glancing at the descending stone, he figured there were less than twenty seconds before it met the floor.

He spotted a vine growing out of the dirt floor in front of him. Extending his left arm as far as he could, he snatched at the vine and then seized it with both hands. Indy grinned with relief as he began to pull himself up, but then the dirt loosened around the vine, causing it to snake out of the floor. Indy gasped as he slid back into the pit — but kept his grip on the vine. Desperate and determined, he reached for the vine hand over hand until his body was out of the pit, then he dived for the rapidly diminishing gap between the floor and the base of the stone slab. As Indy rolled under the gap, he grabbed the whip that Satipo had abandoned, taking it with him as he tumbled into the passage he'd traveled through earlier, the one in which Forrestal had died.

Indy quickly coiled his whip, then heard a loud noise echo from somewhere above his position. He turned to leave the passage, but stopped fast when he nearly stumbled into Satipo.

Like the grotesque masks within the temple, Satipo's eyes and mouth were wide open. But unlike the masks, his expression was frozen with terror. Sharp spikes protruded through his body. He had ignored every caution, and his greed had led him to die just as Forrestal had.

Indy looked down at the ground at Satipo's feet. There, as expected, he found the gold idol lying in the dirt. Indy picked it up, and then turned to face the dead man one last time. "Adiós, Satipo."

Indy headed out of the passage and was only a few steps away from Satipo's corpse when he heard a loud shifting of stone and dirt from behind, followed by an increasingly loud rumbling noise. He stopped to glance back, then gasped as he saw what was coming. A huge, spherical boulder came roaring around a corner of the passage, just above Indy's position. Indy realized instantly that the boulder had been form-fitted to travel through the passage until it blocked the exit.

Indy turned and ran as fast as he could. Behind him, the boulder gained speed as it traveled down the inclined passage. Not even the stalactites that had formed over the years could slow the boulder's velocity. It smashed into them, and launched the spiked rocks like missiles in all directions.

Indy scrambled and ran faster through the twisting, tubular passage, pumping his legs harder to outrun the boulder. Up ahead, he saw a shimmer of light through a haze of thick cobwebs. He dived through the webs to reach the light, and then found himself tumbling down and out of the mouth of the cave. A moment later, the boulder slammed home into the passage's end, sealing the temple's entrance.

Gasping for air and covered with torn cobwebs, Indy was still clutching the gold idol when his tumbling body came to a stop outside the temple. But when he looked up from the ground, he realized he was not alone.

There were three Hovitos warriors in full battle paint. One warrior held a bow and had an arrow trained on Indy, and the other two held spears at the ready. Then Indy looked to his right and saw even more warriors. Some carried spears and bows, and the others had blowguns. From Indy's sprawled position, he was fairly certain there were well over two-dozen warriors, and he was their only target.

Turning his head, Indy saw even more warriors to the left. He was completely surrounded. He was also surprised to see his former guide, Barranca, standing before one of the warriors. Before Indy could comprehend the blank expression on Barranca's face, the warrior behind Barranca gave a slight shove, and Barranca's body teetered and fell forward, landing face-first against the jungle floor. There were over a dozen arrows in the dead man's back.

A shadow fell over Barranca's prone corpse. The shadow belonged to a lean man with a charming smile who was dressed in a safari outfit that included calf-high leather boots, tailored khakis, and a pith helmet. He stepped casually toward Indy, who remained seated on the ground.

Speaking with a French accent, the man said, "Dr. Jones. Again we see there is nothing you can possess which I cannot take away." The man extended his open right hand, waiting for Indy to place the idol in it. The man added, "And you thought I'd given up."

Indy knew the man. He was René Emile Belloq, a mercenary archaeologist who worked for private collectors. They'd had several encounters since the 1920s, and Indy had nothing but disrespect for him. Although Indy had never been able to prove it, he was certain that Belloq had plagiarized his paper on stratigraphy while completing his Masters in Archaeology at the Sorbonne. Since then, Belloq had made a steady and profitable career by taking advantage of other people's hard work.

Still on the ground, Indy eased his hand to his right hip and started to pull his gun from its holster. Seeing his action, all the Hovitos took a step forward, keeping their weapons trained on him. Indy glanced at the Hovitos, then slowly turned his gun handle-forward and handed it to Belloq. As winded as he was, Indy could smell something foul. He realized Belloq was wearing cologne in the jungle.

Taking the gun and transferring it to his left hand, Belloq said, "You choose the wrong friends. This time it will cost you." Belloq extended his right hand again.

Indy shifted his body slightly and drew the gold idol out from under his jacket. As he handed the idol up to the man who loomed over him, he said, "Too bad the Hovitos don't know you the way I do, Belloq."

"Yes, too bad," Belloq said with a smile. "You could warn them, if only you spoke Hovitos." Then Belloq turned away from Indy and dramatically raised the idol high over his head. Having drawn the natives' attention to the idol, Belloq snapped off a few words in Hovitos. His announcement prompted all the natives to prostrate themselves on the ground and bow their heads.

Indy didn't know what Belloq said, but knew better than to stick around and ask. With the natives bowed and Belloq's back turned, Indy took his chance to flee, sprinting toward the edge of the clearing near the temple ruins.

The natives heard Indy's receding footfalls and raised their heads to see his running form. Then they looked to Belloq, who made two sharp hissing sounds as he signaled the Hovitos to pursue the fleeing man and kill him. As the warriors ran off, Belloq held the idol out before him, gazed into the idol's eyes, and laughed defiantly.

Indy heard Belloq's laughter as he ran through the jungle. He didn't like the sound of that laugh. He wasn't crazy about the sound of the many running feet behind him either. And so he did what any archaeologist in his situation would do. He ran faster.

Indy ignored the spears, darts, and arrows that whizzed past his body. He barely glanced at the stone statue of the gaping demon as he raced past it, and didn't stop to pet the donkeys that his guides had roped off less than an hour earlier. He just kept running past the trees and down the hillside, heading back to the river where Jock, the pilot he'd hired, would be waiting with the plane.

What if Jock hadn't waited? Indy didn't even want to think about that possibility.

For a moment, Indy thought he'd lost the warriors, but then another barrage of sharp-tipped projectiles sailed past his shoulders. As his legs carried him away from a tight cluster of trees, he saw the river in front of him. Then he saw Jock's amphibious, tandem two-seat biplane on the river, and then he saw Jock, wearing his familiar short-sleeve blue shirt — the one with AIR PIRATES on its back — and a New York Yankees baseball cap. Jock was standing on one of the plane's pontoons.

There was still a lot of ground to cover between himself and the river. Not sure if Jock could even hear him across the distance, Indy desperately shouted, "Jock! Start the engines! Get it up!"

Did he hear me? Indy was still running hard, but from what he could see, Jock was still just standing on the pontoon. *What's he doing? A jig?* Then Indy noticed a slender line projecting out from Jock's arms and realized with mounting frustration that his pilot was fishing — and seemed to have something on the line.

"Jock!" Indy screamed even louder. "The engines! Start the engines, Jock!"

Jock tossed his fishing pole, abandoning his catch, and scrambled into his plane's cockpit. He fired up the engines just as Indy arrived at a rocky ledge that loomed over the edge of the river. The warriors were still right behind him, and there was nowhere left to run.

Long vines dangled down from the trees that grew around the ledge. Indy grabbed a vine and swung out into the air and over the water, then let go. He splashed down near the plane, which Jock guided closer to his position.

The warriors ran down to the river's edge, and fired their weapons in Indy's direction. Without losing his hat or his life, Indy swam for the plane, grabbed hold of the closest pontoon, and climbed into the cockpit in front of Jock. Jock increased speed as he steered his plane up the river, and he was well out of range of the warriors' weapons as the plane lifted up into the sky.

Indy sunk back into his seat and let the air run over him. Every muscle hurt. He was fairly certain he'd bruised a couple of ribs, but wasn't sure whether that happened at the pit where Satipo had left him to die or during his race from that enormous boulder. He felt even worse about the idol. It was bad enough that'd he'd lost it, but that he'd lost it to a jerk like Belloq made him feel positively lousy. But there wasn't much he could do about it, not now anyway.

Suddenly, Indy jumped in his seat. He'd felt something shift against his legs, and when he looked down, he saw a huge boa constrictor on his lap. Indy's face contorted with an expression of loathing, and he had to fight the incredible urge to jump out of the airborne plane. Squirming in his seat, he turned his head back to snarl, "There's a big snake in the plane, Jock!"

"Oh, that's just my pet snake, Reggie!" Jock responded amicably.

"I hate snakes, Jock!" Indy shouted back as he clenched his fists. "I hate 'em!"

"Come on," Jock said disparagingly. "Show a little backbone, will ya?"

The plane soared off over the dark jungle. As Reggie flopped down around Indy's ankles, Indy made a mental note: *Never fly with Jock again!*

CHAPTER THREE

*L*ess than a week after his adventure in Peru, Indiana Jones was back to his classroom at the prestigious Marshall College in Connecticut. His room was inside an ivy-covered brick building with high windows. On his cluttered desk, several archaeological statues and relics and a stack of old books rested beside a globe of the Earth. Behind the desk, Indy stood before a blackboard and used a stick of white chalk to write letters as he read his writing aloud.

"'Neo,' meaning 'new,'" he said, "and 'lithic'—"

Indy paused to check his spelling, which prompted giggles from the students seated behind him. "I-T-H-I-C—" he continued, "meaning 'stone.'" He underlined the word NEOLITHIC, then turned to face the class.

Wearing a three-piece tweed suit, British-manufactured eyeglasses with gold-filled frames, a fresh haircut, and a clean shave, Indy looked very much the buttoned-down professor and barely resembled the rugged man who'd so recently escaped from the temple of the Chachapoyan warriors. However, it seemed that his glasses did little to disguise his handsome features, as almost every one of his female students was gazing at him dreamily.

Indy gestured to a map he'd already drawn on the board beside NEOLITHIC and said, "All right, let's get back to this site: Turkdean Barrow, near Hazelton. Contains a central pas-passage and three chambers . . ."

Having stumbled over the word *passage*, Indy realized his mind wasn't really on the class. But he'd given this lecture before and knew it well enough, so he just kept talking, and pointed to the map on the blackboard to show where some relics had been removed from Turkdean Barrow. "Don't confuse that with robbing," he said,
"in which case we mean the removal of the contents of barrow."

Just then, the classroom door opened and a distinguished-looking middle-aged man wearing a dark pinstripe suit stepped in from the hallway. The man left the door open as he moved without a word to stand against the wall, where he caught Indy's eye. Indy paused for a moment when he realized the man was his old friend Marcus Brody, but because class wasn't over yet, he returned his student's attention to the map on the blackboard.

"This site also demonstrates one of the great dangers of archaeology," Indy continued. "Not to life and limb, although that does sometimes take place. No, I'm talking about folklore. In this case, local tradition held that there was a golden coffin buried at the site, and this accounts for the holes dug all over the barrow and generally poor condition of the find." Indy pointed to a rectangular chamber on the map and added, "However, chamber three was undisturbed. And the undisturbed chamber and the grave goods that were found in another, uh . . ."

Indy was distracted by one of his female students. Like the others, she had been wearing an almost worshipful expression as she'd watched him. But as his gaze had just momentarily met hers, she'd smiled playfully and closed her eyes, and Indy saw that the word LOVE was written on her right eyelid, and YOU on her left eyelid. When her eyes flashed open again, Indy stammered, ". . . in the area, give us a r —"

Wondering if his own eyes were playing tricks on him, Indy found himself staring back at the girl. She lowered her eyelids again and held them a moment longer than the first time so the professor could clearly read the two words: LOVE YOU. Then she opened her eyes again.

"Uh . . . reason to da —" He tore his gaze from the girl with the lettered eyelids and stammered, ". . . to, uh, to-to date this, uh, find as we have."

Just then, a bell rang to signal that class was over. Still standing before the blackboard, Indy raised a hand to keep the students seated and said, "Um, any questions, then?" He was relieved when no one answered. "No? Okay, that's it for the day, then." As the students picked up their books and began filing out of the class, he pointed to another note he'd jotted on the blackboard and said, "Um, don't forget Michaelson, chapters four and five, for next time. And I will be in my office on Thursday, but not Wednesday."

A young male student, wearing a V-neck sweater and a bow tie, hung back for a moment, waiting for the other students to leave, but then he noticed that the man in the pinstripe suit had remained in the room. Marcus Brody quickly assessed that the student appeared agitated or anxious, and that he probably wanted to talk to Indy, or rather to Dr. Jones, about his grade. The student shifted nervously from one foot to the other, but when he realized Brody wasn't about to leave, he lowered his gaze and headed for the door. The student shot a quick sidelong glance at Indy as he placed a green apple on

Indy's desk before he stalked off, following his class-mates out of the room.

Alone in the room, Indy and Brody looked at each other. Brody walked over to the desk beside Indy and picked up the apple.

"I had it, Marcus," Indy said. "I had it in my hand." Indy held out his right hand and clutched at the empty air.

"What happened?" Brody said as he casually examined the apple.

"Guess."

Polishing the apple against the sleeve of his suit, Brody gave a slight chuckle as he looked up at Indy, then said, "Belloq?"

"You want to hear about it?"

"Not at all," Brody said with a smile as he dropped the apple into his jacket pocket. "I'm sure everything you do for the museum conforms to the International Treaty for the Protection of Antiquities."

Unable to stop thinking about his loss of the gold idol, Indy said, "It's beautiful, Marcus." Then he quickly added, "I can get it. I got it all figured out. There's only one place he can sell it: Marrakesh. I need two thousand dollars. Look —"

As Indy opened a desk drawer and removed a white cloth bag, Brody leaned against the desk and said, "Listen to me, old boy. I brought some people to see you."

Oblivious to Brody's words, Indy said again, "Look." He removed two small artifacts from the white bag. "They're good pieces, Marcus." He handed the best piece to Brody, and said yet again, "Look."

"Indiana . . ." Brody sighed, realizing that Indy was completely fixated with the idea of recovering the idol. Indy handed Brody the second piece and Brody said, "Yes, the museum will buy them as usual, no questions asked." Looking at the two pieces more carefully, Brody added with obvious admiration, "Yes, they *are* nice."

"They're worth at *least* the price of a ticket to Marrakesh," Indy insisted.

"But the people I brought are important," Brody said, "and they're waiting."

Staring blankly at Brody, Indy said, "What people?"

"Army Intelligence," Brody said as he placed both of the pieces that Indy had given him into his jacket pockets, and then began walking slowly for the door. As Indy grabbed a large leather-bound book, his briefcase, and some rolled documents, Brody continued, "They knew you were coming before I did.

Seem to know everything. They wouldn't tell me what they want."

"Well, what do I want to see them for?" Indy said as he followed Brody out of the classroom and into the corridor. "What am I, in trouble?"

Brody shrugged his shoulders and grinned.

A few minutes later, in a large lecture hall that was lined with oak-paneled walls, and tall, stained-glass windows, Brody introduced Indy to the two men from U.S. Army Intelligence, Colonel Musgrove and Major Eaton. Musgrove was a lean, middle-aged man with gray hair who wore a dark three-piece suit and a red bow tie. Eaton was a stout fellow with a strong handshake, a wisp of a mustache, and a receding hairline; he wore a pale blue two-piece suit and dark blue necktie. Musgrove carried a briefcase. Eaton didn't.

After the introductions were made, Brody suggested they be seated on the platform at the front of the lecture hall, where a table and some chairs had been set up for them near a two-sided blackboard. As they mounted the steps up to the platform, Eaton said, "Yes, Dr. Jones, we've heard a great deal about you."

"Have you?" Indy said as he deposited his bag and book on the table.

Eaton said, "Professor of archaeology, expert on the occult, and, uh, how does one say it? Obtainer of rare antiquities."

"That's one way of saying it," Indy said. Gesturing to two chairs beside the table, he said, "Why don't you sit down? You'll be more comfortable."

"Oh, thank you," Eaton said as he took a seat.

"Thank you," Musgrove echoed as he sat beside Eaton. Looking at Indy, he added, "Yes, you're a man of many talents."

Indy didn't know how to respond to that, but he grinned sheepishly. Out of the corner of his eye, he noticed that Brody was standing to his left, leaning against a podium that stood near the table, as if he wanted to keep some distance between himself and the seated men. Indy decided to remain standing, too.

Facing Indy, Eaton said, "Now, you studied under Professor Ravenwood at the University of Chicago."

Noting that Eaton had made a statement, not asked a question, Indy replied, "Yes, I did."

Eaton said, "You have no idea of his present whereabouts?"

"Uh . . . well, just rumors, really." Glancing at Brody, Indy added, "Somewhere in Asia, I think. I haven't really spoken to him for ten years. We were friends, but, uh . . . had a bit of a falling out, I'm afraid."

"Mmm," Eaton said.

Indy didn't like the way the conversation was going and wondered if he'd told the men too much information. He wondered if they knew about the falling-out between him and Abner Ravenwood, and what had caused it. Marcus said they seemed to know everything, so Indy guessed they probably had some idea.

Trying to put Indy at ease, Musgrove said, "Dr. Jones, now you must understand that this is all strictly confidential, eh?"

"I understand," Indy said, still wondering what the men were getting at.

"Uh ..." Musgrove began, then cleared his throat and looked aside to confirm that no one else was in the lecture hall. Returning his attention to Indy, he said, "Yesterday afternoon, our European sections intercepted a ... a German communiqué that was sent from Cairo to Berlin. Now, to Cairo —"

Eaton interrupted, "See, over the last two years, the Nazis have had teams of archaeologists running around the world looking for all kinds of religious artifacts. Hitler's a nut on the subject. He's crazy. He's obsessed with the occult. And right now, apparently, there's some kind of German archaeological dig going on in the desert outside of Cairo."

Musgrove removed a document from his briefcase and said, "Now, we've got some information here, but we can't make anything out of it, and maybe you can." Musgrove traced the words on the document with his finger as he read them aloud: "*Tanis development proceeding. Acquire headpiece, Staff of Ra, Abner Ravenwood, U.S.*"

Indy looked to Brody, and Brody's eyes beamed. Clearly amazed by the communiqué, Indy rapped the edge of the table with his knuckles and said, "The Nazis have discovered Tanis."

Eaton said, "Just what does that mean to you, uh, Tanis?"

Marcus began, "Well, it —"

"The city of Tanis," Indy interrupted, unable to contain his enthusiasm, "is one of the possible resting places of the Lost Ark."

"The Lost Ark?" Musgrove said with a quizzical expression that was shared by Eaton. The two men remained seated, but leaned forward with rapt attention.

"Yeah, the Ark of the Covenant," Indy said. "The chest the Hebrews used to carry around the Ten Commandments."

"What do you mean, 'commandments'?" Eaton said with a slightly impatient edge to his voice. "You're talking about *the* Ten Commandments?"

"Yes, the actual Ten Commandments," Indy said. "The original stone tablets that Moses brought down out of Mount Horeb and smashed, if you believe in that sort of thing."

Eaton eased back in his chair and glanced at Musgrove, whose wide-eyed, open-mouthed expression suggested he was either stunned or baffled. Indy said, "Any of you guys ever go to Sunday school?"

Musgrove said, "Well, I . . ."

"Oh, look," Indy interrupted, and began gesturing with his hands as he explained. "The Hebrews took the broken pieces and put them in the Ark. When they settled in Canaan, they put the Ark in a place called the Temple of Solomon."

"In Jerusalem," Brody noted.

"Where it stayed for many years," Indy continued. "Until, all of a sudden, whoosh, it's gone."

Eaton said, "Where?"

Indy said, "Well, nobody knows where or when."

"However," Brody said, "an Egyptian pharaoh —"

Remembering the pharaoh's name, Indy interrupted, "Shishak."

Brody nodded, and then quickly continued, "Yes ... invaded the city of Jerusalem right about 980 B.C., and he may have taken the Ark back to the city of Tanis and hidden it in a secret chamber called the Well of Souls."

Eaton raised his eyebrows. "Secret chamber?"

Brody nodded, then said, "However, about a year after the pharaoh had returned to Egypt, the city of Tanis was consumed by the desert in a sandstorm that lasted a whole year. Wiped clean by the wrath of God."

Eaton smiled slightly as he shifted in his chair, looked to Musgrove and said, "Uh-huh."

While Eaton turned to re-examine the communiqué, Musgrove gestured with his right hand to Brody and Indy, and said reassuringly, "Obviously, we've come to the right men. Now, you seem to know, uh, all about this Tanis, then."

Indy shook his head. "No, no, not really," he said, stepping away from Brody and the seated men to stand beside the blackboard, which was covered with physics equations. "Ravenwood is the real expert. Abner did the first serious work on Tanis. Collected some of its relics." Indy turned and glanced back at Brody. "It was his obsession, really." Then he looked to Eaton and Musgrove and added, "But he never found the city."

Still looking at the communiqué on the table before him, Eaton said, "Frankly, we're somewhat suspicious of Mr. Ravenwood. An American being mentioned so prominently in a secret Nazi cable."

"Oh, rubbish," Brody said. "Ravenwood's no Nazi."

Pointing to the incriminating communiqué, Musgrove said, "Well, what do the Nazis want him for, then?"

Indy stepped over to the table and said, "Well, obviously, the Nazis are looking for the headpiece to the Staff of Ra and they think Abner's got it."

Lifting his gaze to meet Indy's, Eaton said, "What exactly *is* a headpiece to the Staff of Ra?"

"Well, the staff is just a stick," Indy said. Gesturing with his hands to convey that the staff's length might be taller or shorter than his own height, he said, "I don't know, about this big, nobody really knows for sure how high . . . and it's . . ." He turned to the equation-covered blackboard, rotated the board to its unmarked side, and pulled a chalk stick from his jacket pocket. "It's capped with an elaborate headpiece in the shape of the sun," he said as he drew a circle on the board, "with a crystal in the center." Dragging a line down below the circle to represent the staff, he continued, "And what you did was, you take the staff to a special room in Tanis, a map room with a miniature of the city all laid out on the floor, and if you put the staff in a certain place, at a certain time of day, the sun shone through here —" Indy drew a diagonal line from the top of the blackboard to the center of his drawing of the headpiece, "and made a beam that came down on the floor here." He extended the diagonal line down through the headpiece, and then tapped the end of the line. "And gave you the exact location of the Well of Souls."

Looking from Brody to Indy to make sure he had their information straight, Musgrove said, "Where the Ark of the Covenant was kept, right?"

"Which is *exactly* what the Nazis are looking for," Indy said emphatically.

Eaton said, "What does this Ark look like?"

Pocketing the chalk, Indy said, "There's a picture of it right here." He moved over to the table and carefully unfastened the latches that sealed the leather-bound book he'd carried from his classroom. Opening the book, he found the page he was looking for, and then he lifted the book and positioned it on the table so Eaton and Musgrove had a better view. Indy said, "That's it."

Eaton and Musgrove rose from their seats and gazed down at the book's open pages. At the top of the right-hand page, there was an engraving, an illustration of a biblical battle. Indy had learned most of the details about the illustration from Abner Ravenwood. The picture showed a battle between the Israelites and an opposing army. At the forefront of the Israelite ranks, four hooded men carried the Ark of the Covenant, a gold chest that was crowned by two sculptured angels. The four men were not actually touching the Ark, but carried it by holding two long wooden poles that passed through rings in the corners of the Ark. Brilliant jets of light appeared to issue from the Ark, and pierced the ranks of their vanquished opposition, who were represented in various states of agony and death.

Studying the dramatic image, Eaton muttered, "Good God."

"Yes," Brody said, "that's just what the Hebrews thought."

Pointing to the streaks of light that extended from the Ark, Musgrove said, "Uh, now, what's that supposed to be coming out of there?"

Indy answered, "Lightning . . . fire . . . power of God or something."

Indy turned away from the three men who remained leaning over the book, and walked back to the blackboard to look again at his own drawing of the Staff of

Ra. Behind him, Eaton said, "I'm beginning to understand Hitler's interest in this."

"Oh, yes," Brody said as Indy left the blackboard and returned to his side. "The Bible speaks of the Ark leveling mountains, and laying waste to entire regions. An army which carries the Ark before it . . . is invincible."

Brody looked at Indy. Indy looked away, chewing on his own thoughts. Abner Ravenwood had certainly believed that the Ark of the Covenant existed, though Indy had his doubts. But if it *did* exist, he didn't want it to fall into the hands of the Nazis. Not because he believed that some old chest could possess mystical, deadly power, but because historic artifacts belonged in museums, not in the collection of a crazy dictator.

Indy had another motivation. He didn't know how Abner had gotten mixed up with Nazis, but if his former friend and mentor were in a jam, then he wanted to do something about it. But would Abner want his help? Somehow, Indy doubted that, too.

Still, the more he thought about the Ark of the Covenant, the more he realized he was hooked on finding it.

CHAPTER FOUR

*I*t was early evening as a black sedan with whitewall tires came to a stop in front of a small brick house near Marshall College. Marcus Brody, wearing a fedora, got out of the car and walked to the house's front door. Out of habit, he removed his hat before he rang the doorbell.

Indy opened the door. He was wearing an open, faded-red robe over his pants and T-shirt, and he stared hard at Brody's face. Brody's expressions often betrayed his thoughts, and from his slightly smug grin, Indy was all but certain of what had transpired since their meeting with Eaton and Musgrove earlier that day. As Brody stepped into the foyer, Indy aimed a finger at him and said, "You did it, didn't you?"

Brody smiled broadly. "They want you to go for it."

"Oh, Marcus!" Indy said, clapping his friend on the back as they walked into the adjoining study, where the far wall's built-in shelves were crammed with books and Indy's own small collection of artifacts.

Brody went to a chair in front of Indy's cluttered desk, placed his hat on it, and said, "They want you to get ahold of the Ark before the Nazis do, and they're prepared to pay handsomely for it."

"And the museum?" Indy said as he tied off his robe's fabric belt. "The museum gets the Ark when we're finished?"

"Oh, yes," Marcus said with conviction. After all, that's what Eaton and Musgrove had guaranteed.

Indy took Brody's hand and vigorously shook it. "Oh," Indy sighed, almost overwhelmed by the situation. Releasing Brody's hand, he stepped over to a coffee table where he had an open bottle of champagne and two glasses, one already filled. As he poured a glass for Brody, he looked at his friend and said with amazement, "The Ark of the Covenant."

"Nothing else has come close," Brody said as he took the glass.

Raising his own glass, Indy said, "That thing represents everything we got into archaeology for in the first place."

They clinked their glasses together, then Brody took a sip from his glass while Indy nearly downed his own in one gulp. "Mmm," Indy said, then returned his glass to the table and walked over to a closet and pulled out his battered suitcase.

Seating himself on the arm of the small sofa beside the coffee table, Brody said, "You know, five years ago, I would've gone after it myself. I'm really rather envious."

"I've got to locate Abner," Indy said as he set the suitcase down on top of a dresser and popped it open. "I think I know where to start." He walked back to the closet and grabbed his leather jacket and his coiled bull-whip. Looking away from Brody, he tossed his belongings into the suitcase and tried to sound casual as he said, "Suppose she'll still be with him?"

"Possibly," Brody said, "but Marion's the least of your worries right now, believe me, Indy."

Indy turned around to face Brody, whose gentle smile wasn't so easy to read at the moment. Indy said, "What do you mean?"

"Well," Brody said, "I mean that for nearly three thousand years, man has been searching for the Lost Ark. Not something to be taken lightly." Brody's smile faded, and his expression became gravely serious. "No one knows its secrets. It's like nothing you've ever gone after before."

Indy laughed and slapped Brody on the back as he moved past him, heading for the desk on the other side of the room. "Oh, Marcus. What are you trying to do, scare me? You sound like my mother. We've known each other for a long time. I don't believe in magic, a lot of superstitious hocus-pocus." Bending down behind the desk, he opened a drawer and removed something wrapped in cloth. Carrying the wrapped object away from the desk, he continued, "I'm going after a find of incredible historical significance. You're talking about the bogeyman. Besides, you know what a cautious fellow I am."

Indy opened the cloth to reveal his revolver, a .45 Smith & Wesson Hand Ejector, Second Model. He tossed the gun into the suitcase. As far as he was concerned, his packing was done and he was ready to go.

Traveling by a series of planes from Connecticut to California, Indy eventually arrived in San Francisco, where Pan American Airways had recently inaugurated the first passenger flights across the Pacific Ocean. The aircraft that awaited him in San Francisco's harbor was a Martin M-130 *Clipper*, a four-engine flying boat with an interior that resembled a compact luxury liner in every way. The round-trip ticket to Manila cost over $1,400, and Indy was happy to let the United States government pay for it.

Wearing a dark blue suit and his fedora, Indy walked down the pier that extended alongside the docked *Clipper*. He paid no special attention to the man in the gray trench coat who preceded him past the uniformed steward and onto the plane. The steward, who'd met Indy on a previous flight, saw Indy approach and said, "Nice to see you again, Dr. Jones."

"Thank you," Indy said. Keeping his hat on, he boarded the plane.

Indy climbed the circular staircase that led up to the passenger compartment, which had two seats on each side of a narrow aisle. The ceiling was low enough to prompt him to duck his head. As he made his way to his seat, the steward re-emerged with a tray of drinks. Indy would have responded by saying, "No, thank you," but the noise from the plane's engines was so loud that he just shook his head as he lowered himself into his seat by a window on the starboard side.

Indy looked out the window. Even though he was traveling as fast as the government's money could carry him, it would still be days before he reached his destination. The *Clipper* would make overnight stops at Hawaii and Wake Island before reaching the Philippines, and then he would proceed to Nepal. Bracing himself for the long trip, he loosened his necktie, slouched back in his seat, tilted his hat down over his forehead, and closed his eyes.

A few seats behind Indy, the man in the trench coat lowered his copy of *Life* magazine. Narrowing his gaze through wire-framed eyeglasses, he looked in Indy's direction. The man had been keeping track of Dr. Jones for most of the day. It hadn't been easy getting a ticket on the *Clipper* on such short notice, but the man was most resourceful.

He was a Nazi spy.

CHAPTER FIVE

*T*he renowned archaeologist Abner Ravenwood had done a fine job of making Nepal sound good to his daughter, Marion. He had described the beauty of the Himalayas, and told her they would be staying in Patan, which was widely considered the most beautiful of the three royal cities in Nepal's Kathmandu valley. But as events had turned out, they found their way to the wilder outskirts of Patan, where Abner purchased The Raven, a rough-and-tumble saloon and inn made of rickety wood and a few crumbling stone walls.

At first, it wasn't all that bad. Abner had arrived with numerous objects from his own collection of ancient artifacts, some of which he used for barter. The Raven certainly wasn't a dull place, what with the colorful locals, hikers, and shady characters who stumbled in. There were even a few customers who paid their tabs regularly, just so they could sit on a bench at one of the half dozen tables to warm themselves around the open fireplace and have a drink of the locally brewed *chaang* or distilled *rakshi*.

But then Abner had left Marion in charge of the place while he went off searching for clues and relics that might lead him to the Ark of the Covenant. Instead, he died in an avalanche, and Marion wound up inheriting a saloon that no one else wanted to buy in a country that was landlocked between China and India.

In other words, Marion Ravenwood was stuck in Nepal.

And so it was, on a frigid, windy night in 1936, that Marion found herself sitting in The Raven after closing time, staring at the remains of the evening's drinking competition. A burly, overconfident hiker named Regan had wandered into the bar at nightfall, looking for a challenge, and Marion spotted the chance to supplement her meager income. It wasn't long before Regan's friends were dragging his unconscious body out the door, leaving Marion with the winnings — and a tabletop littered with glasses to clean.

Marion counted the crumpled bills in her hand while The Raven's silent, brawny bartender, Mohan, went outside to collect firewood. The cash would keep The Raven running for another few weeks, but wouldn't get her to the nearest seaport, let alone back to the United States. Not that anyone was waiting for her to come home.

She pocketed the money, then picked up a pair of cold glasses and held them against her temples as she squeezed her eyes shut. Although the drinking contest hadn't affected her disposition much, it had given her a throbbing headache. Standing with her eyes closed and her back to the door, she did not see a man's shadow fall across the far wall as he entered The Raven.

"Hello, Marion," said a deep, familiar voice from behind her.

Still pressing the shot glasses to her temples, Marion turned to face Indy. He was wearing his fedora and leather jacket, and the stubble on his face suggested that he hadn't shaved for at least five days. The Raven's fireplace was blazing behind him, which accounted for his shadow on the wall as well as the warm glow that seemed to radiate from his back. Marion stared at him for a moment, then flung the two glasses away from her head so they smashed against the floor.

Indy didn't flinch.

Then Marion sighed and smiled, as if she were slightly embarrassed by her reaction at seeing Indy after so many years. "Indiana Jones," she said in a sardonic tone. Moving her hands to her hips, she continued smiling as she said, "Always knew someday you'd come walkin' back through my door. I never doubted that. Something made it inevitable."

Indy smiled sheepishly as Marion approached slowly. She was still beautiful, although a bit harder looking now. He was glad to see that she didn't seem at all angry with him. As she came to a stop in front of him, she said, "So what are you doing here in Nepal?"

Turning his face away from Marion, Indy glanced around The Raven. "I need one of the pieces your father collected." But when he looked back to Marion, her right fist was already flying and, before he could duck, it connected hard against his jaw.

Indy's head snapped to the side as he took the hit. He rocked on his feet but didn't fall as his own right hand came up reflexively to stroke his chin and make sure nothing was broken. Because of the way Marion had smiled at him, he'd actually forgotten for a moment that something had already been broken a long time ago: her heart.

"I learned to hate you in the last ten years," Marion spit out as she moved away from him, stepping closer to the fireplace.

Lowering his hand from his bruised jaw, Indy said, "I never meant to hurt you."

Marion snapped, "I was a child. I was in love. It was wrong and you knew it."

Indy was unable to meet her intense gaze. As he stepped over to the bar and leaned against it, he said, "You knew what you were doing."

"Now I do!" Marion snarled. "This is my place! Get out!"

Just then, The Raven's door opened, allowing a sudden blast of wind to enter along with Mohan, who backed in with an armload of firewood. In Nepalese, Marion spoke to Mohan, who placed the wood beside the open door before he stepped outside again, shutting the door behind him.

Despite Marion's command, Indy made no move to leave. Turning to look her straight in the eye, he said, "I did what I did. You don't have to be happy about it, but maybe we can help each other out now."

Turning her back on Indy, Marion walked over to the table that supported what was left of the evening's activities. As she began gathering up the empty glasses and loading them onto a tray, Indy continued, "I need one of the pieces your father collected." Gesturing with his hands as he spoke, he said, "A bronze piece about this size, with a hole in it, off center, with a crystal. You know the one I mean?"

"Yeah," Marion said as she carried the glasses-laden tray to the bar. "I know it."

This conversation is going nowhere, Indy thought. Impatient, he said, "Where's Abner?"

Averting her gaze from Indy, Marion said, "Abner's dead."

For a moment, Indy was speechless. He felt as if he'd been punched again, only this one hurt more than the one that came from Marion's fist. After all, bruises heal, but dead people stay dead. Moving to the bar, he leaned close beside Marion, who still wouldn't look at him. He said, "Marion, I'm sorry."

Marion shook her head. "Do you know what you did to me, to my life?"

"I can only say I'm sorry so many times."

Marion jerked the tray she'd been gripping and the glasses went flying and crashing onto the bar and floor. Turning to glare at Indy, she snapped, "Well, say it again, anyway."

As Marion carried the tray back to the table, Indy said, "Sorry."

"Yeah, everybody's sorry," Marion said as she picked up the remaining glasses. "Abner was sorry for dragging me all over this Earth looking for his little bits of junk. I'm sorry to still be stuck in this dive." Returning to the bar, she added, "Everybody's sorry for something."

Hoping to get Marion off the subject of her anger and sorrow, Indy said, "It's a worthless bronze medallion, Marion. You going to give it to me?"

"Maybe," she said. "I don't know where it is."

"Well, maybe you could find it," Indy said as he reached inside the breast pocket of his leather jacket and pulled out a thick wad of paper money. Holding it up so Marion could see it was American currency, he said, "Three thousand bucks."

Marion eyed the money in his hands. "Well, that will get me back," she allowed, "but not in style." She turned her back to Indy again.

"I can get you another two when we get to the States," Indy said. Irritated by the way Marion was deliberately ignoring him, he grabbed her upper arm and spun her around to face him. "It's important, Marion," he said. "Trust me."

Either Marion didn't trust Indy or she just wanted to belt him again, for her hand suddenly lashed out toward his face. This time, Indy caught her wrist, and he gently placed the money into her hands. "You know the piece I mean," he said. "You know where it is."

Marion wrapped her fingers around the bills and laughed. Smiling at Indy, she said, "Come back tomorrow."

Cautious, Indy said, "Why?"

"Because I said so, that's why." She feinted another jab at Indy's chin, and he caught that one, too. Taking the money, she turned and sat down at the edge of a table.

"Ha!" she said as Indy headed for the door. "See you tomorrow, Indiana Jones."

Indy paused for a moment after he'd opened the door, and then stepped outside. After he'd gone, Marion walked over to another table that was littered with empty glasses that encircled a candlestick that had been carved from a twisted branch. She sat down on a bench beside the table, then slipped her fingers into her blouse to remove the circular bronze medallion she wore on a chain around her neck.

A single candle burned in the candlestick on the table, and its flame danced in the drafty saloon while Marion examined the medallion. A winged bird dominated the design, with the bird's head positioned slightly above the center. An inset crystal took up most of the bird's head, and Egyptian letters ringed the outer edge. Marion knew that this piece was the headpiece of the Staff of Ra, at least that's what her father had believed. For some reason, she hadn't wanted to sell it off after her father died, maybe because she knew it was one of his most prized pieces. Or maybe just because it reminded her of him.

She still missed her father. Every lousy day since he'd died.

Holding the headpiece in one hand and her money in the other, Marion grinned. If she wanted to, she could sneak off with the money *and* the headpiece. As far as she was concerned, that would serve Indy right. However, she doubted that she'd be able to hide for long. If he could find her in Nepal, he could find her anywhere.

She studied the headpiece again. Why was Indy so interested in it, anyway? To her surprise, she suddenly felt torn over the idea of selling it, especially to Indy. Fortunately, she had the night to think it over. She didn't really want to part with the last tie to her father, but she didn't want to stay in a stinking saloon in Nepal for the rest of her life either. If it served as her ticket back home, then at least one of her father's relics had been good for something.

Lifting the headpiece by its chain, Marion draped it over the carved candlestick and got up from the table. She carried the three thousand dollars to the bar, where she found the cigar box that served as The Raven's cash register, and placed the bills into the box. Then she reached into her pockets to remove her winnings from the drinking contest and put those notes into the box, too.

Marion had just lowered the lid on the cigar box and was stepping away from the bar when The Raven's door swung open with a loud thud into the wall. Pausing mid-step, she turned to see four men standing in the doorway. Two of the men wore black hats with matching leather trench coats and gloves; one wore round wire-frame eye-glasses, and the other had a black mustache. Marion knew these two weren't locals. The other two looked vaguely familiar: a Nepalese in ratty-looking clothes and a tall, broad-shouldered Mongolian. It was the bespecta-cled man in black who had pushed open the door. Although he wasn't a remarkably tall man, he was the most looming presence among his group.

"Good evening, *Fraülein*," said the bespectacled man as he stepped into the saloon. His German accent was unmistakable. And like the man on the Pan American *Clipper* who had tracked Indiana Jones to Nepal, he was a Nazi agent.

CHAPTER SIX

Although the bespectacled man with the German accent did not introduce himself to Marion Ravenwood, his name was Arnold Toht. He was a top agent of the Gestapo, the official secret police of the Nazi Party, and his mission was to secure the headpiece to the Staff of Ra on behalf of the *Führer*, Adolf Hitler. Toht was skeptical of the supernatural, and had no idea whether the head-piece would lead to the Ark of the Covenant, or whether the Ark would help the Nazis defeat their enemies. However, Toht was also a most devoted Nazi, and he would do anything to please the Führer, especially if it allowed him to use his skills as an interrogator. For when it came to getting information out of people, Toht was considered something of an expert.

"The bar's closed," Marion said dismissively to the four men who stood in The Raven's doorway. She could sense that they were a dangerous bunch, and the bespectacled man's accent didn't score points with her either.

But the men ignored her and stepped into the saloon. A smile twitched across Toht's pale face, and his words tumbled out in a shivering stammer. "We . . . we are . . . not thirsty."

Marion wasn't sure if the German was genuinely shivering or if he always talked that way — as if he were trying not to giggle at some incredibly sick joke. On some dim instinctive level, she wanted to run, but she refused to let anyone frighten her in her own bar. Without displaying a trace of fear, she walked casually toward them and said, "What do you want?"

"The same thing your friend Dr. Jones wanted," Toht said as Marion lit up a cigarette. "Surely he told you there would be other interested parties."

"Must've slipped his mind," Marion said.

"The man is . . . nefarious," Toht said between shivers as he came to a stop before Marion. Then, as if he had finally warmed up, he added smoothly, "I hope, for your sake, he has not yet acquired it."

Marion said, "Why, are you willing to offer more?"

"Oh, almost certainly," Toht said. "Do you still have it?"

Marion blew smoke straight into the German's face.

Irritated, he responded with a low cough. Stepping away from the man and moving behind the bar, Marion said, "No. But I know where it is."

The big Mongolian began to follow Marion. She saw his movement out of the corner of her eye and knew he was moving up behind her, but she kept her gaze on the bespectacled German on the other side of the room.

Ignoring Marion, Toht moved toward the small pile of flaming logs in the open fireplace, which consisted of four baked-brick columns that supported an exposed stone chimney that rose up through the ceiling. Bending down to inspect the logs, Toht said, "Your fire is dying here." He removed his right glove, then reached out with his bare right hand for the iron poker resting at the edge of the fireplace. "Why don't you tell me where the piece is right now?"

"Listen, Herr Mac," Marion said in a low voice as she leaned against the bar. "I don't know what kind of people you're used to dealing with, but nobody tells me what to do in my place."

"*Fraülein* Ravenwood," Toht said as he pushed the tip of the poker against a burning log, "let me show you what I am used to."

Toht snapped off a monosyllabic command, and the Mongolian grabbed Marion from behind. "Take your hands off me!" Marion shouted as he lifted her off her feet. Glasses shattered as the brute shoved her over the bar, where the Nepalese was waiting for her on the other side. "Take your lousy hands off!" The Mongolian moved quickly around the bar, then took Marion from the Nepalese and pinned her arms behind her back with one vise-like hand.

And then Marion noted that the German with the creepy voice had stepped away from the fireplace. He was holding the smoldering poker, and its tip glowed bright orange. He wasn't smiling anymore. The other man in a black trench coat — the one she assumed was also German — stood off to the side, staring at her blankly.

"Wait a minute," Marion said, and heard the fear in her own voice as the man with the poker stepped toward her. "Wait," she gasped. "I . . . I can be reasonable."

"That time is past," Toht said flatly. As he moved closer to Marion, she saw that his face was now covered with sweat. It seemed as if the fireplace had not only warmed his features, but thawed his evil nature.

"You don't need that," Marion said as her eyes went wide and she trembled in the Mongolian's grip. The man with the poker moved closer to her, so close that she could smell his foul breath. She gasped, "Wait . . . I'll tell you everything."

"Yes," he said, leaning even closer, "I know you will." He raised the poker so that its tip was just inches from Marion's face. She kept her eyes open and focused on the tip, and Toht had no doubt that she knew what he was about to do, that the red-hot poker would be the last thing she ever saw before she died.

But Toht was wrong.

From out of nowhere, there came a loud cracking sound. Toht felt a sudden jolt along his arm as the end of a bullwhip wrapped around the poker. He reflexively opened his fingers as the whip yanked the poker aside and flung it across the saloon, where it landed beneath a heavy curtain against the far wall.

Toht moved fast, grabbing Marion and shielding himself with her body as he turned to face his unseen attacker. He found himself staring at Indiana Jones.

Indy held his bullwhip in his right hand and his revolver in his left. His hands were now covered by leatherwork gloves, and there was a thin layer of snow on the brim of his hat. Keeping the barrel of his gun leveled at the man in the black trench coat who was holding Marion, Indy said, "Let her go."

Behind Indy, the heated poker suddenly caused the curtain to ignite and burst into flames. Toht's eyes flicked to the fire, then back to Indy.

Indy heard a ratcheting sound as the other guy wearing a black trench coat raised a machine gun. Indy spun fast and shot at the man with the machine gun. The machine gunner stumbled back, pumping bullets into The Raven's ceiling, but he didn't go down. Marion wrenched herself from Toht's grip, then dived for cover beside the bar.

Indy fired at the machine gunner once more, then rapidly switched his revolver to his right hand and shoved his whip into his jacket as he scrambled for cover. Indy threw himself into a stone-walled alcove that ended at the saloon's back door as a hail of bullets hammered at the walls and ricocheted past his body. But leaving through the back door was not an option he could consider — not with Marion still in danger.

The bullets were still flying as Indy poked his head and gun arm out fast to fire three more rounds back at his attackers. He only managed to hit some bottles on the bar, which exploded and sent glass flying everywhere, but he quickly noted the positions of the four men as well as Marion before ducking back into the alcove to reload his Smith & Wesson.

Marion was crouched down beside the far end of the bar. The Mongolian and the machine gunner had both moved behind the bar, and the fiend who'd been holding the poker now held a pistol that he'd pulled from the depths of his trench coat. The Nepalese was still out in the open, with just the open fireplace between him and Indy.

Indy risked more bullets and another glance from the alcove to see the Nepalese grab hold of a wooden table and flip it onto its side so he could use the tabletop's thick planks as a shield. The Nepalese's action sent more glasses and bottles crashing to the floor, as well as the candlestick around which Marion had left the headpiece.

From her crouched position beside the bar, Marion saw the headpiece hit the floor. No one else had taken notice of the bronze relic amidst the shards of broken glass and spilled liquor, but she knew there was no way she could reach it without getting caught in the crossfire.

Then Marion saw a machine gun sail over the bar and land in the Nepalese's waiting hands. She realized the Mongolian must have tossed it to him. She wanted to shout out and warn Indy, but if anyone else heard her over the roar of gunfire, she knew they wouldn't hesitate to turn their weapons and cut her down.

While the Mongolian began firing a machine pistol in Indy's direction, the Nepalese lowered himself behind the overturned table. Bracing the machine gun's barrel on the tabletop's edge, he fired a stream of bullets into the wall near Indy.

Indy ducked back into the alcove to avoid the barrage. Several agonizing seconds later, the Nepalese stopped firing, and Indy guessed the machine gun had jammed or run out of bullets. As good as Indy was with a gun, he was pretty sure he couldn't get a straight shot at the Nepalese as long as he was behind the overturned table. So when Indy leaned out fast from the alcove and fired two precisely aimed rounds, he didn't aim for the Nepalese. He aimed for the stack of logs in the fireplace.

Struck by Indy's bullets, the burning logs tumbled out of the fireplace and onto the floor in front of the overturned table. The logs ignited the puddle of spilled liquor around the table, and the Nepalese dropped his machine gun as his liquor-soaked clothes caught fire. Suddenly engulfed in flames, the Nepalese rose screaming from behind the table.

From the doorway, Indy saw he now had a clear shot at the Nepalese. He fired, killing him instantly. Marion screamed as the Nepalese fell to his knees and collapsed in front of her. The other machine gunner and the Mongolian continued firing at the far doorway, keeping Indy pinned in the alcove.

There were now several small fires burning in the saloon, and all were spreading fast. Glancing around to make sure she wouldn't be spotted, Marion reached out from beside the bar to grab the non-burning end of one of the logs that Indy had launched from the fireplace. Moving slowly, she held the log with one hand as she raised her head to peek over the bar. Sure enough, the Mongolian was still firing at Indy. As bullets continued to whiz overhead, Marion edged her way along the floor behind the bar.

Still braced in the doorway, Indy winced as one of the machine gunner's bullets creased the left sleeve of his leather jacket. Indy stumbled back and tucked his body into a smaller alcove to the left of the back door. Because of his position, Indy was forced to transfer his revolver to his left hand to return fire. But just as he prepared to squeeze off another round, the door behind him swung open and slammed against his outstretched arm. Indy groaned as the door met his arm and he accidentally fired at the ceiling. Then he felt a pair of massive hands grab him from behind and slam him into the stone wall beside the doorway.

The man who had burst through the door to attack Indy was a hulking, bearded Sherpa, even larger than his Mongolian ally behind the bar. At the sight of the Sherpa, the Mongolian and the machine gunner held their fire.

As Indy was being beaten by the Sherpa, Marion — still clutching the smoldering log — stealthily moved up behind the Mongolian. She raised the log with both hands, and then brought it down hard over the back of the Mongolian's head. The big man slumped forward, then collapsed unconscious to the floor.

Toht and the machine gunner didn't see the Mongolian fall or notice Marion duck back down behind the bar — their attention was on the Sherpa and Indy. They stepped away from the burning walls as the Sherpa lifted Indy off his feet and carried him toward the bar.

Dazed from the beating and the smoke that now filled The Raven, Indy somehow managed to hang on to his gun with his left hand even as the Sherpa slammed him into the bar. As Indy let out another pained groan, the Sherpa forced his head down so that his left cheek was pressed upon the countertop, which was slick with spilled alcohol.

Out of the corner of his eye, Indy spied Marion down behind the bar, fumbling with the Mongolian's fallen machine gun. The Sherpa hadn't noticed her — he had his head turned to gaze down the length of the bar. Indy followed the Sherpa's gaze and saw the machine gunner standing beside the bald, spectacled man.

There was a single unbroken bottle of liquor resting on the countertop near Toht, who had picked up a small, burning stick from the floor. He deliberately knocked the bottle over as he held out the burning stick, and the liquor caught fire as it flowed across the bar's surface toward Indy.

Indy knew it was only a matter of seconds before the creeping flames reached his head. Craning his neck to face Marion, he wriggled the fingers of his right hand as he ordered, "Whiskey!"

Without hesitating, Marion snatched a bottle of whiskey from the counter near her head and handed it to Indy. He grabbed the bottle by the neck and twisted his body toward the Sherpa, gaining just enough leverage to smash the bottle against the Sherpa's head.

The Sherpa fell back from the bar, pulling Indy away from the flames that now covered the bar's surface. Indy still clutched his revolver in his left hand and tried to angle it at his opponent, but the Sherpa pinned Indy's left arm with one hand and wrung his neck with the other. Indy gasped for air as the Sherpa leaned over him, forcing him down on top of a nearby table.

Toht and the mustachioed machine gunner stepped forward. Apparently, Toht did not trust that the Sherpa would kill Indy, or maybe he just wanted to be rid of the Sherpa as well, for he tilted his head to the machine gunner and commanded, "Shoot them. Shoot them both."

The Sherpa must have understood Toht's words or sensed that he had been betrayed, for his grip slackened on Indy as he turned his gaze to the two Germans. As the machine gunner stepped forward and prepared to fire, the Sherpa suddenly pushed Indy's gun arm forward, allowing Indy to squeeze the trigger four times in quick succession.

Toht jumped aside as Indy's bullets slammed into the machine gunner. As the gunner toppled to the floor, the Sherpa pulled Indy from the table. For a moment, Indy thought he had at least a temporary truce with the Sherpa, but then he realized the Sherpa was trying to wrestle the revolver from Indy's hand. They tumbled to the floor, punching and kicking.

Trying to stay out of range of the fighting men, Toht trotted over behind the overturned table that the Nepalese had used earlier as a shield. It was then that Toht caught sight of the bronze medallion that rested in a tangle of glass and splintered wood beside the table's charred surface. He knew at once that it was the headpiece of the Staff of Ra. While Indy and the Sherpa continued their fight, Toht reached forward, wrapping his fingers around the headpiece. He was so eager, it hadn't occurred to him that the bronze headpiece might be hot.

There was a sickening searing sound as Toht lifted the metal medallion and smoke issued from his palm and between his fingers. His face contorted with intense pain and he screamed in agony as he released the sizzling bronze, letting it fall back to the floor. He continued to shriek as he clutched his wounded hand and — wanting nothing more than to escape the burning saloon and find relief in the snow — ran straight for the nearest window and dived through it, breaking glass as he went.

Back in the saloon, the fight for the gun had taken Indy and the Sherpa to the floor beside the fireplace. Indy managed to shove the Sherpa's arm into nearby flames, forcing him to release his grip on the gun. A moment later, Indy was on his feet, but so was the Sherpa, his right sleeve now ablaze.

There was a whoosh of flame as the Sherpa swung his burning arm at Indy's head. Indy ducked and drove his fist into the Sherpa's face. The Sherpa's head tilted back slightly from the hit, so Indy hit him again. Harder.

The Sherpa stumbled. Seizing his chance, Indy grabbed a heavy table, lifted it high off the floor, and swung it down over the Sherpa's back. The table broke apart, and the Sherpa fell in a heap.

Remembering Marion, Indy turned toward the bar. But instead of Marion, he found himself facing the Mongolian that Marion had clobbered earlier. Given the angry glare on the Mongolian's face and the pistol he had aimed at Indy, it appeared that Marion hadn't clobbered the man hard enough.

Indy flinched as he heard the gunshot. He knew the Mongolian couldn't have missed him, not at such close range, so he was surprised when he didn't feel the sudden pain of a gunshot wound. But then he saw the blood trickle out of the Mongolian's mouth, just before the man's body went limp and he collapsed for the very last time ever. And as the Mongolian slid down behind the bar, Marion was revealed, standing at the back of the bar with a gun in her hands.

Indy smiled and cocked his head. As the saloon burned all around them, Marion lowered the pistol and yelled, "My medallion!"

She found the headpiece of the Staff of Ra on the floor, and used a balled-up handkerchief to pick it up. Then Indy grabbed her and pulled her through the front door of The Raven, or rather what was left of it. Less than three minutes had passed since Indy had used his whip to make the German drop the red-hot poker, and now Marion's saloon was reduced to burning timbers.

The wind howled and tore at Indy and Marion as they stumbled away from the fire. Indy glanced around, searching for any sign of danger. As far as he could see, it was just Marion and he outside.

"Well, Jones," Marion shouted over the wind, "at least you haven't forgotten how to show a lady a good time!"

He reciprocated, shouting back, "Boy, you're something!"

"Yeah?" Marion shouted back. "I'll tell you what! Until I get back my five thousand dollars, you're going to get more than you bargained for!" Holding out her medallion for Indy to see, she said, "I'm your partner!"

CHAPTER SEVEN

*I*ndiana Jones and Marion Ravenwood didn't talk much on the Air East Asia flight that carried them from Nepal to Karachi, the major port and capital city of the Sind province, and both of them slept during most of their subsequent flight from Karachi to Baghdad. But after they left Baghdad, Indy told Marion a little more about his plan and about Sallah, the man they were going to meet in Cairo.

Sallah was a professional excavator who had worked with Indy on previous archaeological digs. He had a large family, was beloved by his friends, and had a fondness for the music and lyrics of Gilbert and Sullivan. It was easy for Indy to talk about Sallah, and Marion found herself eager to meet him.

Sallah did not disappoint. He stood six-foot-two, weighed over 220 pounds, and had a baritone voice that somehow made him seem even larger. With open arms,

he welcomed Indy and Marion into his home, and introduced them to his wife, Fayah, and their children. There
wasn't an unhappy face in the house. Just as Indy had
expected, Marion liked Sallah and his family
immediately.

After Marion changed into a clean white blouse
and skirt, she and Fayah followed Indy and Sallah up to
the balcony on the roof of Sallah's house. It was warm
outside, too warm for Indy to wear his leather jacket,
which he had left inside along with his weapons and his
hat. Most of the balcony was open to the bright sun, but
there was also a shaded area with wicker furniture under
a canopy, where Sallah's children were huddling around
a table.

While Indy hung back near the canopy, the other
adults carried their drinks to the edge of the balcony,
which overlooked the rooftops of the city. Gesturing
dramatically at the whitewashed buildings that surrounded his own, Sallah said, "Cairo! The city of the
living. But a paradise on Earth!"

What a ham, Indy thought as his mouth broke into a
broad smile. He was always glad to see Sallah.

A burst of giggles escaped from the table nearby.
Indy turned, looking toward the children, their giggles
now transformed into peals of squealing laughter. Fayah

stiffened as she approached the table. "Silence!" she said. "Why do you forget yourselves? What is this?"

The children parted. On the middle of the table, beside a bowl of fruit, stood a Capuchin monkey wearing a red vest. The small monkey chittered as it looked up at Fayah.

Fayah gasped. "Where did this animal come from?"

Marion and Sallah joined the group and watched as the monkey played with the fruit. When the monkey rolled on its back and knocked over a drink, Marion smiled as she leaned over the monkey and said, "Oh . . . oh, no."

The monkey leaped for Marion. She laughed nervously as it scrambled up her arm and onto her shoulders. As it wrapped a furry arm around her cheek, she glanced at Indy and said flatly, "Cute. What an adorable creature."

Fayah smiled and said, "Then it shall be welcome in our house."

"Oh, well, no," Marion responded quickly as the monkey tugged at her hair and hugged her neck. "You don't have to keep it here just because of me!" The monkey was still hugging her when she noticed Indy. He was smiling fondly as he looked at her.

Indy thought, *I can't believe I'd forgotten how beautiful she is.*

Marion smiled back, and then she turned, carrying the monkey away from the table. Remembering their manners, the children became suddenly orderly as they followed Marion to sit and play with the monkey beside the canopied area, leaving the wicker chairs for Indy and Sallah.

As Fayah poured more wine for the men, Indy picked up a lemon from the fruit bowl and began peeling it with a small knife. He looked across the table to Sallah and said, "I knew the Germans would hire you, Sallah. You're the best digger in Egypt."

"My services are entirely inconsequential to them," Sallah said without modesty. "They've hired or shanghaied every digger in Cairo. The excavation is enormous! They hire only strong backs and they pay pennies for them. It's as if the pharaohs have returned."

Still working on the lemon, Indy said, "When did they find the map room?"

"Three days ago," Sallah said. "They have not one brain among them." He paused. "Except one. He is very clever. He's a French archaeologist."

French? Indy looked up from the lemon he'd been cutting. He said, "What's his name?"

"They call him 'Bellosh,'" Sallah said.

Indy laughed at this, and Sallah looked at him curiously for a moment before he joined in. When the laughter ended, Indy leaned back in his chair, looked at Sallah and said, "Belloq. Belloq."

"The Germans have a great advantage over us," Sallah said gravely. "They are near to discovering the Well of Souls."

"Well," Indy said as he reached into his pocket, "they're not going to find it without this." He pulled out the headpiece to the Staff of Ra and held it up for Sallah's inspection, letting him see the symbols etched into its surface. As Indy handed the headpiece to Sallah, he asked, "Who could tell us about these markings?"

"Perhaps a man I know can help us," Sallah said as he examined the piece closely. Then, and somewhat hesitantly, Sallah added, "Indy . . . there is something that troubles me."

"What is it?"

Sallah leaned forward and planted his elbows on the table. "The Ark," he said. "If it is there, at Tanis, then it is something that man was not meant to disturb. Death has always surrounded it. It is not of this Earth."

Not of this Earth? Because Indy wasn't superstitious, he didn't know how to respond to that. For all he knew, the stories about the Ark of the Covenant were just folklore. He wanted to put Sallah at ease, but the truth was that there did exist a great deal of danger surrounding the Ark that *was* of this Earth, namely that Belloq and the Nazis were searching for it, too.

Indy remained determined to find the Ark before the Nazis. But if anything bad happened to Sallah, he would never forgive himself.

While Sallah went to meet a man and find out about the markings on the headpiece, Indy and Marion agreed to go do some shopping. Marion changed into a white blouse and red, loosely fitted trousers that were gathered at the ankle. Leaving his leather jacket at Sallah's house, Indy put on his hat and gun belt, tucked his whip beneath his shoulder bag, and went out with Marion into the crowded streets of Cairo. They didn't go alone.

"Do we need the monkey?" Indy said as the little creature jumped from the back of his neck to Marion's. "Huh?"

Walking alongside Indy past the vendors who were selling everything from food and brass goods to rugs and jewelry, Marion grinned. "I'm surprised at you, Jones. Talking that way about our baby." She patted the monkey as it shifted to her right arm, then she added, "He's got your looks, too."

"And your brains," Indy grumbled.

"I noticed that," Marion said, smiling at the monkey, which she realized was actually female. "She's a smart little thing." Turning to Indy to make sure he'd heard her, she repeated, "*Smart.*" Then she laughed as the monkey tugged at her ear.

Without warning, the monkey leaped from Marion's arm, landed on the cobblestone street, and began to scurry away on its hands and feet.

"Hey!" Marion shouted after the fleeing monkey. "Wh-Where're you going?!" The small monkey darted past the feet of some other shoppers, then vanished from sight.

"She'll be all right," Indy said, happy to be rid of the monkey. As Marion stared off down the street, trying to sight the monkey, Indy held a small, open bag in front of her and said, "Have a date."

Marion glanced at the bag, and then removed a small piece of the dried fruit without looking at it. Her attention was still focused on down the street, where she'd last glimpsed the monkey.

"Come on," Indy pressed. He wasn't about to spend the rest of the day chasing down the animal, so he tugged Marion by the arm and repeated, "Come on."

"Okay . . ." Marion said, still looking away from him for some sign of the monkey.

"Marion," Indy said as he gave another tug.

Marion suddenly noticed the dried fruit in her hand. Having been preoccupied when she'd taken it from Indy, she now looked at it and said, "What's this?"

"It's a date," Indy said. "You *eat* 'em."

Indy and Marion moved on without the monkey. They were among the few people on the street who weren't wearing long white or black robes. Most men's heads were wrapped in *keffiyeh*, folded square cloths that were the traditional headdress of Arab men, and the women wore shawls called *hijabs*. But as the man in the fedora and the woman in red trousers found themselves relaxing slightly in each other's company, it didn't occur to either of them how much they stood out in the crowd.

Not far from where it had abandoned the two Americans, the runaway monkey made its way around the corner of a building. There was a bearded man sitting on the building's front steps. The man wore a turban and a black patch covered his right eye. The monkey climbed up next to the man and tugged at his arm.

To his employers, the man was known simply as the Monkey Man. He was a mercenary spy who hired himself out to the highest bidder. And right now, the Monkey Man and his Capuchin accomplice were working for the Nazis.

Carrying his monkey on his shoulder, the Monkey Man stepped into a nearby building where he found two men wearing tan suits. The men were Germans, Nazi agents. Seeing them, the Monkey Man raised his left hand and rasped, "Sieg heil!"

One of the Germans raised his right hand and said quietly, "Ja."

Seeing the German's casual salute, the monkey snapped its own right arm up and squawked. Without thinking, the German found himself raising his right hand again, returning the monkey's salute, as the other German muttered, "Heil Hitler."

"Sieg heil!" the Monkey Man rasped again, then he pointed past the two Germans, directing them to the area where Indy and Marion were headed. With that gesture, his clandestine meeting with the Germans was over.

While the Monkey Man and his monkey ran off to catch up with Indy and Marion, the two Germans went to an upstairs room with a balcony that overlooked the busy street. Inside the room, a group of robed men, their heads wrapped in black *keffiyehs*, waited for the Germans. The men had already been provided with a description of the American couple. After the Germans sighted Indy and Marion walking along the street below, one of them turned from the balcony and nodded.

The waiting men filed out of the room and building, taking their swords with them.

CHAPTER EIGHT

*M*oving on without the monkey, Indy and Marion continued their tour through Cairo's narrow, dirt-covered streets. Soon, Indy's arms were loaded with small cloth bags filled with various goods. They exited an arched passage that led to more vendors, and were walking past a horse-drawn cart that was loaded with straw when Marion said, "How come you haven't found some nice girl to settle down with, raise eight or nine kids like your friend Sallah?"

"Who says I haven't?" Indy said.

"Ha ha! I do!" Taking another date from the bag she now carried, Marion said, "Dad had you figured out a long time ago. He said you were a bum."

"Oh, he's being generous." Indy had been joking, sort of, but as soon as the words were out of his mouth, he regretted them. Abner Ravenwood *was* being generous, and Indy hadn't completely absorbed the fact that his former friend and mentor was dead.

"The most gifted bum he ever trained," Marion continued, oblivious to Indy's embarrassment. Stopping in front of a table that displayed cooking pots, an assortment of handmade figurines, and rugs, Marion said, "You know, he loved you like a son. It took a whole lot for you to alienate him."

"Not much," Indy said. "Just you."

Suddenly, Indy sighted three white-robed men running fast from the nearby arched passage. They wore black *keffiyehs*, which they had wrapped around their heads so only their eyes were visible. The man in the lead drew a long dagger from the sash at his waist as he ran straight for Indy. The one at the rear held a sword.

Indy dropped the packages, letting them fall to the ground between him and Marion. Unaware of the rapidly approaching men, Marion stooped down to pick up the fallen bags. Just as she crouched, the man with the dagger sailed over her stooped form and into Indy.

Dodging the dagger, Indy grabbed his attacker's weapon hand, and then shoved him hard, knocking him into the guy with the sword. As both men fell, Indy turned to help Marion, who'd been seized by the swordsman.

Indy belted that guy in the face, and he, too, went down.

As the surrounding shoppers and vendors backed away to watch the fight, Marion just stood there for a moment, looking stunned. But when she saw that the man who had grabbed her was trying to get up again, she picked up a fallen metal container and began beating him over the head.

Another dagger-wielding, face-concealed attacker leaped into the fray. He lunged at Indy, who blocked the attack and struck back, sending the man crashing against the nearby merchant's table. As Indy turned, the other men he had just knocked to the ground were up again, and joined by yet another man. One of them came at Indy with a length of wood, but Indy jumped back as the fiend's swing went wide and smashed into one of the other fighters. Indy socked the guy with the wood, knocking him into the man behind him.

Before any of his attackers could get up again, Indy spun around to see that Marion was still pounding the metal container against the head of the man who'd grabbed her. As that man finally collapsed beside the merchant's table, Indy seized Marion by the shoulders and turned her to face him as he shouted, "Marion, get out of here!" Then he gazed past Marion's head and his eyes went wide.

"Duck!" Indy shouted, pushing Marion down in front of him as he threw a punch over her head. An instant later, his clenched fist smashed against the nose of still another masked attacker, who had been coming up behind Marion with a sword raised high over his head. The surrounding onlookers gasped as the Arab dropped the sword and fell backward onto the street.

Marion stood up, looking even more stunned. Indy wanted to get her out of harm's way, but as he saw one of the fallen attackers begin to rise, he realized the fight wasn't over yet. He shoved Marion aside, then turned and kicked hard at the Arab's stomach.

So far, Indy had counted at least six masked men. Before he could wonder if there were more on the way, he felt a seventh slam into him and found himself being thrown against a nearby fruit stand. Indy pushed himself away from the stand and threw his elbow hard into the man's face. There was an ugly sound at the impact, and the seventh attacker fell.

Two more masked swordsmen lunged, quickly taking his place. Indy threw himself back toward Marion, and one swordsman accidentally drove his sword straight through the other's stomach. As Marion grimaced at the carnage, Indy grabbed her wrist and yanked her after him.

As the astonished crowd shouted, Indy and Marion ran back up the street, toward the arched passage where the straw-filled cart remained parked. Indy threw Marion into the back of the cart, and then reached for the bullwhip that was coiled behind his shoulder bag.

Uncoiling the whip as he turned away from the cart, Indy saw two of the masked Arabs coming at him. He let the whip loose with a loud crack, forcing the men back. But when he cracked the whip a second time, it got the attention of the horse that was hitched to the cart. The horse shot forward and the cart suddenly lurched away through the passage behind Indy, taking Marion along for the ride.

The horse and cart picked up speed as they traveled out the far end of the passage, with Marion feeling every bump on the road as she flopped against the straw and tried to right herself. Because the cart's wooden sides were higher than Marion's head, she could see only the road behind the cart, and was unaware that she was being watched from the street by two men: a German agent in a tan suit, and a bearded man who wore an eye patch and had a familiar monkey sitting on his shoulder.

The moment that the cart slowed, Marion jumped out and started to run back for the arched passage. She'd run only a short distance when she saw a man sprinting straight toward her. Although he wasn't wearing a black *keffiyeh*, she could tell from his angry, determined expression that he was after her. Marion dashed to the front of the nearest building, where a merchant had hung a net displaying metal pots and pans. The merchant stood speechless as Marion plucked a frying pan from his display and turned to confront her pursuer.

Marion held the frying pan and readied to swing, but her pursuer stopped in his tracks a short distance away. Then he reached behind his back and pulled out a knife, laughing menacingly as he held it out at Marion, who looked aghast.

Then Marion smiled brightly. "Right," she said, before turning on her heel and running with the frying pan still held tightly in her hand.

The attacker continued to chase after Marion, following her into a nearby alley and then through a dark doorway. But a moment after he stepped over the threshold, there was a loud *clang* as Marion whacked him in the head with the pan. He fell back out through the doorway, where he took a second hit as the back of his head struck the cobblestones.

Marion hastily grabbed the unconscious man's ankles and hauled him into the building so his body wouldn't lead his friends after her. But when she ran back into the alley, she saw two white men in suits followed by several masked Arabs approaching from an adjoining alley.

Some large rattan baskets were stacked up alongside a nearby wall. Hoping to elude the approaching men, Marion lifted the lid to an empty basket, climbed inside, and then quickly repositioned the lid over her head.

Her heart was racing as she heard the men run past the baskets. As much as she wanted to go help Indy, she was tempted to stay in the basket until she fully recovered her breath. But a moment later, she heard a strange scratching sound outside her basket, and then something screeched from atop the lid above her head.

It was the little monkey. Though Marion had wanted the monkey to return to her, she wished it had picked a different time. It continued screeching and raising such a ruckus that Marion pressed up against the basket's lid and tried to dislodge the monkey as she whispered loudly, "Shhh! Shhh!"

But the monkey just shrieked louder, which prompted the men who had just ran past Marion's basket to stop and turn around.

Clutching his coiled bullwhip in his right hand, Indy was drenched in sweat by the time he found the cart that had carried Marion away from him. The cart and its horse were resting in the middle of the street, and there were plenty of people walking around, but there was no sign of Marion.

Indy jumped up onto the side of the cart to get an elevated view of the area. Scanning the surrounding streets and the robed pedestrians that flowed over them, he shouted, "Marion!"

No response.

Indy jumped down from the cart. He wondered if Marion had gotten away, and if she were now trying to make it back to Sallah's house. Uncertain of his next move, he'd only taken a few steps away from the cart when the people around him suddenly dispersed.

Sensing trouble, Indy looked to his left and found himself staring across a short expanse of vacated ground at a massive swordsman. The swordsman was clad in black robes and had a scarlet sash around his waist. In his hands, he held an immense scimitar. Facing Indy, the swordsman grinned as he raised his curved blade. His laughter came out in a low rumble, like approaching thunder.

The surrounding expectant crowd went silent.

By Indy's eye, the swordsman stood about twenty feet away from him, which was ten feet beyond the reach of his ready bullwhip. Indy watched closely as the swordsman quickly transferred his scimitar from one hand to the other, chopping at the air and whipping the blade expertly around his body.

Show-off. Indy had no doubt that the swordsman intended to kill him, but he sure was taking his sweet time about it. Worried about Marion, and exhausted from fighting in the oppressive heat, Indy thought, *I don't have time for this.* While the swordsman continued to demonstrate his deadly prowess, Indy wearily shifted his bullwhip to his left hand, then lifted his gun from its holster and fired.

The crowd roared as the swordsman dropped his scimitar and collapsed to the ground. A young man picked up the fallen scimitar and lifted it high above his head as other people danced around him and cheered. Apparently, no one thought Indy had fought unfairly. If the swordsman had been foolish enough to pick a fight with a gunslinger, his death was his own fault.

Looking away from the fallen swordsman as if he had been just a minor distraction, Indy returned his gun to its holster and squinted as he tried to see past the jubilant crowd that surrounded him.

Marion, he thought. *Where are you?*

And then, incredibly, he heard her voice.

"Help!" Marion called out. "Over here, Indy!"

Her voice was muffled — it seemed to be coming from a rattan basket that was being carried on the shoulders of two men who were just beyond the surrounding mob.

The men under the basket were wearing black *keffiyehs*.

"Get out of the way!" Indy snarled as he pushed his way through the crowd. "Move! Move it!" He couldn't be sure why the masked men had attacked him at the market, but given what had happened back in Nepal, he had a feeling Germans were involved.

Indy chased the two basket-carrying men into an alley. He nearly lost sight of them, but then he heard Marion shout again, "Help me! You can't do this to me! I'm an American!"

Indy followed the voice and sighted the men and the basket again. He ran faster. From the basket, Marion cried out, "Indy!"

Indy was only ten strides behind when they turned a corner into another alley. But when he reached the corner, they were gone. Indy stopped, listening intently. A moment later, Marion's muffled voice echoed off the alley walls: "Indiana Jones! Help me, Jones!"

Hoping he was going in the right direction, Indy chased the echoing voice to the end of an alley, where it emptied into a busy intersection. And then he stood there, gaping.

Everywhere he looked, Indy saw men carrying baskets exactly like the one Marion was trapped in. There were literally dozens of them, maybe over a hundred, and they were all moving in different directions. Some of the basket-carriers wore black *keffiyehs*; others wore white. The difference hardly mattered to Indy now. He ran out into the street and knocked the nearest large basket out of the hands of the men who carried it. When that basket's lid slid off and revealed that it contained nothing but folded fabric, the basket's carriers began shouting at Indy. Indy ignored them as he moved fast to upset another basket along with another group of men. That basket yielded more fabric, which tumbled onto the street, so Indy ran to knock over another basket, and then another and another.

Most of the baskets held clothing and fabric. As dozens of angered basket-carriers began shouting at Indy, he suddenly heard Marion's muffled voice again: "Jones!"

Her cry had come from behind, beyond the ring of outraged merchants and laborers that now encircled him. Indy turned and shouted, "Marion!" Thrusting out his elbows, Indy broke past the angry throng at a full run, just in time to sight Marion's basket-carrying captors dart off between two buildings and into another alley.

He bolted after them. Despite their load, the men moved swiftly through the twisting alley, but their unburdened pursuer ran faster. Indy kept his eyes forward as he hurtled over the narrow cobblestone street, and saw the men turn left when they reached an intersecting alley. He followed them, but when he ran out into the intersection, he was greeted by a rapid burst of machine-gun fire.

Bullets hammered into the cobblestones at Indy's feet. He came to a sudden stop, reflexively lifting his arms to shield his body from the bits of stone that the bullets sent flying. He had just a brief glimpse down the length of the street before he spun and doubled back into the alley for protective cover. The glimpse registered that the machine gunner was another man wearing a black *keffiyeh*, and that Marion's captors were carrying her basket toward a truck that was parked outside a small shop. Indy thought he also saw a pair of white men who wore tan suits and fedoras, but he couldn't be sure.

More bullets tore at the buildings around Indy as he drew his revolver and braced himself against the wall in the alley. When the gunfire ceased, he risked a glance down the street and saw the Arabs loading Marion's basket into the back of the truck. And he'd been right — there *were* two men in tan suits. He wondered, *Who're those guys?*

Indy was about to make a run for the truck when he felt hands grabbing at him. A group of beggars, apparently oblivious to the gunfire as well as the revolver held high in Indy's hand, began yammering at Indy, asking him for money. With his free hand, Indy dug into a pocket, grabbed some loose coins, and threw them away from himself, down the length of the alley. As the grateful beggars moved away from him, Indy heard a man's voice yell from the parked truck around the corner. "*Los! Schnell! Schnell!*"

Germans!

Indy heard the truck's engine start. He jumped out of the alley and faced the truck, which was now moving toward him and picking up speed. The masked machine gunner stood on the running board outside the driver's door.

Standing his ground, Indy took careful aim and fired three times at the machine gunner. The gunner screamed as he was hit and fell from the moving truck. As the driver threw the wheel hard to the right to steer away from Indy, Indy took aim again and shot the driver, too.

As the driver's body went slack, his body dragged the wheel further to the right at the same time that his foot jammed down on the accelerator. Out of control, the truck careened down the street before it swerved onto a steep embankment beside a building's loading platform.

The truck's right tires traveled up the incline, and then the entire vehicle flipped over onto its side and skidded to a stop.

Indy was still running for the crashed truck when it erupted into a massive fireball. The blast knocked Indy off his feet, and he groaned as he was tossed back against the outer wall of a nearby building. He realized the truck must have been carrying explosives. As he turned his gaze to the burning truck and rising cloud of black smoke, he also realized something far worse.

"Marion . . ."

He stumbled forward, and then began to run, heading for the truck. But then he stopped running. The explosion and fire had already reduced the truck to a smoldering skeleton of twisted metal. No one could have survived it.

No one.

CHAPTER **NINE**

*I*ndiana Jones sat at a table on a patio. According to the painted letters on the wall behind him, he'd found his way to the Marhala Bar. The Capuchin monkey in the little red vest lay in front of him on the table, right next to Indy's glass and a bottle that was only a couple of pours away from being empty. Indy didn't remember his walk to the bar or ordering the bottle, and couldn't recall whether he had found the monkey or the monkey had found him. None of that seemed to matter very much, not since he'd seen that truck explode.

He knew that the blazing truck must have attracted the local authorities, but he hadn't bothered to stick around and wait for them to show up. Even if they weren't corrupt, they could no sooner bring Marion back from the dead than he could. And so he had just walked away, drifting through the streets and alleys of Cairo until he somehow wound up at the bar. With the monkey.

Marion liked the monkey.

The monkey tugged at Indy's fingers and then sat up. Indy looked down at the animal's upturned face and thought he saw concern in its eyes. He stroked the monkey's little hand with his thumb and thought, *I'll bet you're wondering where Marion is.* Unfortunately, Indy knew the answer to that question.

It's all my fault, he thought for the hundredth time. *If I hadn't gone to Nepal, and then let Marion come to Cairo with me, she'd still be alive.* He'd allowed her to get dragged into this mess, and he hadn't been fast enough to save her life. He had failed her. It was as simple as that.

A shadow fell over Indy's table. He looked up to see two men. One wore a tan jacket to match his pants, the other was in his shirtsleeves and wore glasses. Indy had never seen either of them before.

"Dr. Jones," said the man in the jacket. Then, speaking in German, he told Indy that another man wanted to talk with him inside the bar.

Indy grimaced, and felt a rush of rage sweep over him. He hadn't forgotten the other two men in tan suits he'd seen earlier, by the truck that had carried Marion to her death. One of those men had spoken German, too.

Had those men died along with Marion? Indy didn't know. Were the two men who now stood beside his table Nazis? He wouldn't bet against it.

Indy glanced at the German who had just spoken to him. The man held his left arm at an angle so that his fingers brushed against the lapels of his jacket. Indy had no reason to doubt the man was carrying a gun.

Indy's own revolver was in its holster at his hip. Angered as he was, he made no move for his weapon. Instead, he decided to play along with these men and see where they took him. If they made trouble for him, he was prepared to give it back in spades.

Without a word, Indy rose from the table. He scooped up the monkey and his nearly finished bottle and walked slowly toward the bar's open entrance. The man in the jacket followed close behind.

The smoke-filled bar was a series of white-walled rooms connected by arched doorways. The only signs of modernity were the electric fans that dangled and spun from the ceilings. Most of the patrons were Arabs who sat in small groups around tables and on chairs that were lined up along the walls. A few of them stole cursory glances at Indy as he and the German moved deeper into the bar.

The German guided Indy over to a column where a glowering man stood. Glaring at him, Indy said, "You looking for me?" But the man just laughed in his face and walked away. Then, to Indy's surprise, the German walked off, too, leaving him standing alone with his bottle in one hand and the monkey on his shoulder.

Indy turned around slowly and found the man who had summoned him. The man wore a white suit and a black-banded Panama hat, and was seated at a table, examining a cheap pocket watch.

"Belloq," Indy said.

"Good afternoon, Dr. Jones."

Moving closer to Belloq's table so that he loomed over his adversary, Indy muttered, "I ought to kill you right now."

Belloq shrugged as he put the pocket watch down on the table. "Not a very private place for a murder."

Surveying the other men in the bar, Indy said, "Well, these guys don't care if we kill each other. They're not going to interfere in our business."

"It was not *I* who brought the girl into this business," Belloq said petulantly. Gesturing to an empty chair at the end of his table, he continued, "Please, sit down before you fall down. We can at least behave like civilized people."

Indy put his bottle on the table and sat down in the offered chair. The monkey crawled down from his shoulder, slinked off of his right arm, and then vanished below the table. Watching the monkey's progress, Belloq said, "I see your taste in friends remains consistent."

Seated beside Belloq, close enough to reach out and strangle the smug Frenchman, Indy kept his eyes forward, refusing to meet his adversary's gaze. Indy never felt the talented monkey remove his revolver from its holster, nor saw the animal carry the gun over to the Monkey Man, who stood with some men on the other side of the bar.

Watching Indy intently, Belloq said, "How odd that it should end this way for us, after so many stimulating encounters. I almost regret it. Where shall I find a new adversary so close to my own level?"

"Try the local sewer," Indy said.

Belloq let out a small laugh. "You and I are very much alike," he said as he gave an appreciative nod to Indy. "Archaeology is our religion, yet we have both fallen from the purer faith. Our methods have not differed as much as you pretend. I am a shadowy reflection of you. It would take only a nudge to make you like me, to push you out of the light."

Keeping his eyes averted from Belloq, Indy snarled, "Now you're getting nasty."

"You know it's true," Belloq said with a smooth, confident smile. "How nice. Look at this." He held up the pocket watch he had before him, and dangled it by its chain. Indy gave it a slight glance out of the corner of his eye. "It's worthless," Belloq continued. "Ten dollars from a vendor in the street. But I take it, I bury it in the sand for a thousand years, it becomes priceless . . . like the Ark. Men will kill for it. Men like you and me."

"What about your boss, *der Führer*?" Indy said with obvious disgust. "I thought he was waiting to take possession."

At Indy's mention of the Nazi leader, Belloq's eyes shifted to the nearby Arabs. If they'd understood Indy's words, they didn't seem to care. Returning the watch to the table and his gaze to Indy, Belloq said, "All in good time." Then he leaned close to Indy and added, "When *I* am finished with it. Jones, do you realize what the Ark is? It's a transmitter. It's a radio for speaking to God. And it's within my reach."

Indy had heard enough. Turning his head to stare directly into Belloq's eyes, he said, "You want to talk to God? Let's go see Him together. I've got nothing better to do."

Indy shoved the table forward with his left hand as his right reached for his holster. In the same instant that he discovered that his revolver was gone, there suddenly came from all around him the ratcheting and clicking sounds of dozens of guns being readied, as the surrounding Arabs and even the German in the tan suit whipped out their concealed weapons and aimed them at Indy.

Fortunately, there came another sound, too. "Uncle Indy," a child's voice cried out, "come back home now!"

"Uncle Indy!" another child cried. And while Belloq and the astonished Arabs looked on, a group of smiling children came running into the bar and swarmed over Indy, throwing their little arms around him.

Indy grinned. The children were Sallah's.

Good old Sallah. As bad as the surrounding cutthroats were, Indy doubted that they would fire on a bunch of innocent kids. When the men angled their weapons away from the children and started laughing, Indy was certain of it.

The children held tight to Indy as he rose from his chair. He tossed a defiant glare at Belloq, who said, "Next time, Indiana Jones, it'll take more than children to save you."

Sallah's children maintained their tight cluster around Indy as they escorted him past the laughing Arabs. As they moved toward the exit, Indy found the Capuchin monkey sitting on the edge of a table. He reached out and the monkey climbed up his arm and returned to his shoulder.

Walking away from the Marhala Bar, still surrounded by Sallah's children, Indy saw Sallah himself approaching from his parked blue pickup truck. Looking at Indy, Sallah said, "I thought I would find you there." Then he gestured to his children and said, "Better than the United States Marines, eh?"

Indy picked up the monkey and lowered him through the truck's open window and onto the driver's seat. As he gave one of Sallah's daughters a boost into the back of the truck, he said to Sallah, "Marion's dead."

"Yes, I know," Sallah said gravely as Indy lifted another daughter into the truck. "I'm sorry." Then he added, "Life goes on, Indy. *There* is the proof." With a tilt of his chin, he indicated his children, who were now giggling in the back of the truck.

Neither Indy nor Sallah noticed the monkey peer through the truck's open window. The Monkey Man sat on his motorcycle, which was parked about thirty feet behind Sallah's truck, on the other side of the street. The Monkey Man made a hand signal, commanding his small accomplice to stay with Indy for the time being. The obedient monkey ducked back down into the truck.

"I have much to tell you," Sallah said as he placed his hand on Indy's shoulder. Gesturing to his children again, he said, "First we will take them home, and then I will take you to the old man."

Sallah climbed into the driver's seat while Indy got into the back with the children. Behind them, the Monkey Man started his motorcycle's engine. He would keep a discreet distance as he followed the truck to its destination.

*   *   *

The "old man" that Sallah had mentioned was an astronomer, priest, and scholar in his seventies. Served by a small apprentice named Abu, Imam had a long, gray beard, and lived in a house that was filled with exotic artifacts, hanging lanterns, and wind chimes. The house had a large, open hole in one of its walls that offered a sweeping view over the neighboring rooftops, and allowed Imam to train his antique telescope on the stars that now twinkled in the night sky above Cairo.

The air had grown cool since sundown, cool enough that Indy now wore his leather jacket. He stood in Imam's kitchen and peered out through the back door's intricate latticework to view the alley behind the house. Ever since he and Sallah had left the Marhala Bar, he had the feeling that they had escaped Belloq's clutches just a bit too easily. He didn't think anyone had followed them to the house, but he figured it wouldn't hurt to check the alley anyway. Nothing moved, and all was quiet.

Sallah had promised Indy that he would find a replacement for the revolver that had been snatched from him back at the bar. As capable as he was with a whip, there were times when only a gun would do. Indy wasn't especially sentimental about his old Smith & Wesson, but if he ever caught the thief who'd taken it, he would make that louse pay.

Turning from the back door, Indy saw Abu standing at the sink, rinsing some dates in a colander. After the dates were thoroughly rinsed, Abu tilted the colander and poured the dates into a wooden bowl that he had placed beside a decanter on a round tray on the edge of a nearby table. Indy left the kitchen for the adjoining room, where he found the vested Capuchin monkey now perched on Sallah's shoulder while the old man examined the headpiece to the Staff of Ra. Then Abu followed after Indy, leaving the dates behind.

Lurking in the shadows of the alley outside the kitchen, the Monkey Man watched the figures leave, and then he made his move. He pushed open the back door without a sound and removed a small red bottle from beneath his robes as he stepped over to the kitchen table. He quickly emptied the bottle's clear liquid contents over the bowlful of dates, and then — hearing footsteps approach — turned fast and slipped out the back doorway. He had been inside the kitchen for barely fifteen seconds.

Abu returned to the kitchen carrying two glasses. As he placed them on the tray, he felt a breeze at his back, then turned and saw that the back door was not closed. Had the visiting American left it open? Abu could not recall. He stepped over to the doorway, peeked outside, saw no one, and shut the door.

Abu picked up the tray that held the dates, decanter, and glasses, and carried it into the adjoining room. There, Imam was seated at a low table near his telescope, and used a magnifying glass to inspect the markings on the headpiece.

"I can't figure out how Belloq did it," Indy said to Sallah. "Where'd he get a copy of the headpiece? There are no pictures, no duplicates of it anywhere."

"I tell you only what I saw with my own eyes," Sallah said while the monkey — seeing Abu approaching with the tray — scampered down from his shoulder and onto the floor. Gesturing to the bronze in Imam's hands, Sallah continued, "A headpiece like that one, except 'round the edges, which were rougher. In the center, the

Frenchman had embedded a crystal, and . . . and surrounding the crystal, on one side, there were raised markings, just like that one."

Abu had placed his tray on a table near Sallah. Indy stepped over to the table, reached into the bowl, and picked up a date. Holding it in his hand, Indy turned away from the table and said, "They made their calculations in the map room?"

"This morning," Sallah confirmed as he moved after Indy. "Belloq and the boss German, Dietrich. When they came out of the map room, they gave us a new spot in which to dig, out away from the camp."

"The Well of Souls, huh?" Indy said.

Sallah nodded. Neither noticed that the monkey had climbed up onto the table and picked up a date.

Unexpectedly, Imam looked up from his seat at the low table and exclaimed in his high voice, "Come, come look . . . Look here . . . look." There was excitement in his wise old eyes. Pointing to two chairs on either side of him, he said, "Sit down. Come, sit down."

Reaching into his pocket, Indy pulled out his glasses and put them on. As he took his seat beside Imam, he said, "What is it?"

Pointing to one side of the headpiece, Imam said, "This is a warning, not to disturb the Ark of the Covenant."

"What about the height of the staff, though?" Indy asked. "Did Belloq get it off of here?"

"Yes," Imam replied. "It is here." He dragged a bony finger over the headpiece to indicate the markings in question. Tapping at the markings, he said, "*This* was the old way, *this* mean six kadam high."

"About seventy-two inches," Sallah calculated.

Indy was still holding the date that he'd removed from the bowl and was about to pop it into his mouth when Imam looked at Sallah and said, "Wait!" The single word suddenly left Indy holding his breath as he waited for Imam to continue, and he unconsciously lowered the date away from his mouth as he watched Imam rotate the headpiece to show him the markings on the other side. Translating the markings, Imam read aloud, "*And take back one kadam to honor the Hebrew God whose Ark this is.*"

The translation left Indy and Sallah looking stunned. As a wind blew in through the open windows and made the chimes tinkle, they rose slowly from their chairs and stepped away from Imam. Indy removed his glasses, and then grinned as he looked to Sallah. "You said their headpiece only had markings on one side. Are you absolutely sure?"

Sallah nodded.

"Belloq's staff is too long," Indy said.

Then, at the same time, both Indy and Sallah said, "They're digging in the wrong place."

Sallah laughed, and then clapped Indy's shoulders. Smiling broadly, Sallah began to sing from Gilbert and Sullivan's *H.M.S. Pinafore*, "*I am the monarch of the sea. I am the ruler of the* —"

While Sallah sung, Indy tossed the date high into the air, tilted back his head, and opened his mouth. But before the date could fall back down and into his mouth, Sallah's hand darted out and caught it in midair.

Surprised, Indy looked at Sallah, and then followed his friend's gaze to the rug on the floor, where the little monkey lay dead beside the bowlful of poisoned dried fruit.

"Bad dates," said Sallah.

CHAPTER TEN

*A*rchaeologists believed that the ancient city of Tanis, located in the Nile Delta, was originally founded over 4,000 years ago. Various evidence indicated Tanis had been a commercial city and the northern capital of Egypt for centuries, but had been abandoned in the 6th century C.E. when Lake Manzala threatened to flood the area. The city was indeed flooded, and when the waters dried, most of the structures were buried under silt. Although a few European archaeologists collected statuary from Tanis during the 19th century, most of the site remained unexcavated until 1936, when René Emile Belloq arrived.

Belloq was assisted by numerous German "associates," gun-toting soldiers and guards who maintained a constant watch over the laborers who were hard at work shoveling dirt and sifting through sand. It was a massive operation, and the Germans had set up many tents to accommodate the men and vehicles. In an effort not to draw too much attention to their presence in Tanis, the Germans wore drab uniforms that were without any ornamentation that might reveal their affiliation with the Nazi Party.

Under the command of the Germans, the laborers had already moved tons of dirt. Although Belloq had found the ancient map room, and the Nazis had obtained a representation of at least one side of the headpiece to the Staff of Ra, the Well of Souls remained undiscovered.

Carrying a map of the area that he had rolled into a long, tight tube, Belloq was wearing an open-necked shirt and khaki slacks as he conducted his morning inspection of the excavation site. He was accompanied by Colonel Dietrich, the tall, blond German Wehrmacht officer who was in command of the operation at Tanis, and Dietrich's aide, a younger dark-haired man named Gobler. As the two uniformed officers followed Belloq past a group of laborers, Belloq yelled over his shoulder, "I told you not to be premature in your communiqué to Berlin. Archaeology is not an exact science. It does not deal in time schedules."

"The Führer is not a patient man," Dietrich snapped from behind. "He demands constant reports, and he expects progress! You led me to believe —"

"Nothing!" Belloq exclaimed. "I made no promises. I only said it looked very favorable. Besides, with the information in our possession, my calculations were correct."

Because most of the laborers wore similar garments, neither Belloq nor the German soldiers thought anything unusual of the two men dressed in white robes and *keffiyehs* walking past the metal rails that had been set up for carts to transport loads of sand. One of the men was Sallah, who carried a shovel over one shoulder, and who was officially on payroll for the excavation. The other man was Indiana Jones, who carried a long wooden staff that he used like a walking stick.

Indy surveyed all the activity around them and commented, "Boy, they're not kidding, are they?" Indeed, the laborers seemed intent on leaving no grain of sand unexamined. As Sallah led him over yet another set of rails, Indy said, "What time does the sun hit the map room?"

"At about nine in the morning," Sallah said.

"Not much time then," Indy noted. "Where are they digging for the Well of the Souls?"

"On that ridge," Sallah said, indicating the ridge with a discreet tip of his shovel's handle. Then, tilting his chin to a small hilltop at their right, he added, "But the map room's over there."

Eager to reach the map room, Indy said, "Let's go, come on."

Sallah and Indy climbed up the hill where they had to step over the low barbed wire fence to reach an exposed ring of cut stones that encircled a wide hole: the entrance to the map room. Indy stopped at the edge of the hole, peered down into it, and glanced around to make sure that he and Sallah were not being watched. Then he casually held his wooden staff over the hole and let it fall until it clattered against the floor of the underground chamber.

Sallah tied off one end of a long rope to a metal pole that served as a post for the wire fence, then handed the remaining length to Indy. While Sallah braced himself at the edge of the hole, Indy lowered himself down the rope.

The air was cool in the subterranean interior of the map room, which was lined with elaborate wall coverings and frescoes, all lit by the bright stream of sunlight that flooded in through the hole above Indy. After reaching the floor, Indy gave the rope a tug to let Sallah know he was okay, and then he picked up the wooden staff that he had tossed down. He moved forward into the chamber to examine its most remarkable feature: a meticulous stone model of the city of Tanis as it had appeared thousands of years earlier, when it was still in its glory. On one of the miniature buildings, some inconsiderate German had used red paint to scrawl *nicht stören*, which Indy knew translated as *do not disturb*.

That's where they're looking for the Ark, Indy thought. *Fools*.

Sallah didn't see the two German soldiers approach until they were right behind him. He pretended to ignore them as he moved away from the hole, but when they began shouting and he realized they weren't about to go away, he decided he would have to create a diversion to keep them from discovering Indy.

Because he couldn't very well leave the rope dangling down the hole, where it could only arouse more suspicion, Sallah dragged the rope along after himself as he smiled nervously and stepped over the low barbed wire fence. Then, moving down the hill with the Germans, he deliberately stumbled and rolled to the bottom of the slope, where more soldiers watched him from beside their parked car.

Back in the map room, at the base of the architectural model of Tanis, Indy found a long, flat tablet. The tablet's tiled surface was marked by a series of evenly spaced slots. Indy used his hands to sweep aside the layer of sand that had accrued over the tiles, and he found symbols that indicated the time of year.

He removed a small brush and notebook from his robes, and gently removed more sand from the tiles as he studied the symbols and checked them against his notes. When he found the correct slot for that time of year, he turned his gaze back to the sunlit hole in the ceiling and he grinned. It was now only minutes away from 9:00 A.M., and he was that much closer to finding the Well of Souls.

Reaching into a pocket, Indy removed the headpiece to the Staff of Ra and carefully mounted it onto his staff. As sunlight continued to stream down from above, he positioned the base of the spear into the designated slot on the tiled tablet. And then he waited.

It wasn't long before the sunlight touched the headpiece. Focused through the crystal at the headpiece's center, the sunlight generated a red beam that projected from the crystal to the miniature city. As the seconds ticked by, Indy watched as the red beam traveled slowly across the miniature. When the beam moved over the surface of the building marked *nicht stören*, he realized he'd been holding his breath. He deliberately gulped at the air to avoid getting lightheaded.

The red beam continued to move over the miniature until it reached the center of a high-walled rectangular structure. By some trick of ancient artistry, this one replica seemed to respond to the projected beam, for it suddenly glowed brightly. Beams of unearthly, golden light radiated outwards, illuminating the entire map room. Indy's eyes went wide with amazement as he beheld the radiance.

When the golden light faded, Indy was almost trembling with excitement. Recovering his nerve, he stepped away from the staff, leaving it standing in its slot, and removed a measuring tape from his pocket as he walked over to the miniature buildings. Stretching the tape from the replica that had been so brilliantly illuminated to the one that represented the area where Belloq's men were digging, Indy quickly calculated the actual location for the Well of Souls.

After scribbling a few last notes, Indy removed the staff from its slot and returned the headpiece to his pocket. Then he broke the staff over his raised, bent knee.

Finished with the map room, Indy angled his head to face the hole in the ceiling and whispered, "Sallah." When no response came, he whispered louder. "Sallah!"

Wondering what was keeping his friend from lowering the rope, Indy moved forward so he was standing directly below the hole. A moment later, his head was struck by what felt like a bundle of laundry. He reached to his head to clutch a piece of red fabric that had wrapped around his head and shoulders. As he unfurled the fabric, he was surprised to find a thick black swastika emblazoned in the middle of it. It was a Nazi flag, and it had been knotted to bits of clothing, tunics, and robes to form a makeshift rope.

Looking up, Indy saw Sallah peering down through the hole. Indy knew better than to ask questions. He climbed out of the hole.

Sallah quickly informed Indy of what had transpired while Indy was in the map room. It had taken a good deal of Sallah's cunning to extract himself from the German soldiers, enter a tent filled with various supplies, and steal the fabric necessary to make a new rope. It had also taken some nerve to sneak *back* to the hole outside the map room. Indy was relieved — and grateful that he had a partner as resourceful as Sallah.

As they made their way back across the excavation site, they neared a group of German soldiers dining at a long table. Although Indy's jaw was covered with stubble, he hardly had the swarthy features that characterized most of the Arab laborers, and knew his disguise wouldn't hold up under close inspection. So he lifted the edge of his *keffiyeh* and wrapped it across the lower half of his face.

One of the soldiers stood up beside the table and began yelling in German at Indy. Indy shrugged and pretended that he didn't understand them, but the soldier shouted again, and then another soldier tried to grab Indy's wrist. The soldiers wanted Indy to serve them.

Indy's *keffiyeh* slipped, exposing his face. Although none of the soldiers recognized him, he didn't want to invite their attention either.

Realizing Indy's predicament, Sallah faced the shouting German and said obligingly, "Please, my friend, what is the matter? I fetch the water. I shall get it for you."

Indy didn't want to proceed without Sallah, but he couldn't just stand around the table. Pushing his *keffiyeh* back over his face, he slunk away from the seated soldiers. As he moved off, he heard Sallah tell them, "If you want water, I will get you water. No problem, no problem,"

Indy was still struggling with his *keffiyeh* when four soldiers came marching toward him. Hoping to avoid another confrontation, he turned to his left and ducked into a large striped tent. He had no idea what or who was in the tent, but because its striped exterior was an Arabic design, it seemed like a safer option than other nearby tents, which were standard German military issue. He certainly didn't want to walk into a tent full of soldiers.

Inside the tent's spacious interior, he found a young woman seated on the ground, with her back leaning up against the pole that served as the tent's central support.

A knotted handkerchief gagged her mouth, and her wrists were twisted behind her back, binding her to the pole.

Much to Indy's astonishment, the woman was Marion Ravenwood.

CHAPTER ELEVEN

*G*agged and bound inside the tent, Marion was still wearing the same white shirt and red pants that she'd had on when the Arabs abducted her the day before. The knotted handkerchief bit into the edges of her mouth as she twisted her head to glare at her visitor. There was genuine fear in her eyes, for she did not recognize the man, as his face was mostly obscured by his *keffiyeh*. She struggled against her bonds as he dropped to his knees beside her and tried to hug her. Marion released a muffled scream.

Pulling away from Marion, Indy lifted the end of his *keffiyeh* aside to reveal his awestruck expression. Despite the gag across her mouth, Marion beamed.

"I thought you were dead," Indy gasped as he reached behind her head to untie the gag. "They must have switched baskets." After he removed the gag, he was unable to stop himself from leaning forward to kiss Marion fully on the mouth. She returned the kiss, and then Indy pulled back again to ask, "Are you hurt?"

"No," Marion answered breathlessly. "You have to get me out of here, quick. They're gonna be back any minute." She saw Indy pull out his pocketknife and said, "Cut me loose. Quick."

As Indy reached behind Marion and was about to cut the rope that bound her wrists, she continued, "They keep asking about you. What you know."

Indy leaned back from Marion's bonds. Marion noticed a strange, distant look in his eyes, then felt a pang of panic as he folded the blade back into the handle of his knife and slowly returned it to his pocket.

"What's wrong?" Marion said. "Cut me loose."

Looking into Marion's eyes, Indy said gravely, "I know where the Ark is, Marion."

Surprised, Marion said, "The Ark's here?"

Indy nodded.

"Well, I'm coming with you, Jones," Marion said, wriggling against her bonds. With mounting nervousness, she blurted out, "Get me out of here! Cut me loose! You can't leave me here!"

Indy tried to keep his voice calm, but wound up rattling off quickly, "If I take you out of here now, they'll start combing the place for us." He hoped Marion would understand his reasoning. Unfortunately, she didn't.

"Jones, you've got to get me out of here!" Marion said as Indy picked up the handkerchief he'd only just removed from her face. "Come on, Jones, are you crazy?!"

"Marion, I hate to do this," Indy said as he wrapped the gag back around Marion's mouth, "but if you don't sit still and keep quiet, this whole thing is going to be shot." Marion was still breathing hard but had stopped struggling as he promised, "I'll be back to get you." He kissed her forehead, and then rose quickly to exit the tent.

Marion tried to shout after him, but Indy had tied the gag well, and her cry was muffled.

Shortly after leaving Marion in the tent, Indy reunited with Sallah and informed him that Marion was still alive. Much as Sallah wanted to help Marion, too, he agreed that a premature rescue effort would likely end in their own capture — or worse.

At Indy's request, Sallah procured a tripod-mounted transit, a small rotatable telescope used in archaeological fieldwork to measure angles and distances, and survey structures and areas of land. Although the Germans had a reputation for manufacturing high-quality optical equipment, Sallah pointed out with some amusement that the transit had been cobbled together from an old

American model. Indy figured the Nazis had probably stolen the transit's pieces.

Indy kept clear of the German soldiers as he climbed up a hill that offered a good view of the entire excavation site, and also placed him at an elevation that was approximately the same as the top of the distant, dunelike mound that housed the map room. He set up the transit, and then consulted the notes he had taken in the map room.

Indy peered through the scope and centered it on the barbed wire-surrounded hole that was the map room's entrance. He adjusted the scope's focus, and then slowly swiveled the scope to the left, focusing on the area where Belloq's men were searching for the Ark. He took a reading from the transit, referred once again to a note from the map room, then swiveled the scope again to the left, letting the sights pass over more dunes until he saw what appeared to be a large, undisturbed mound of sand and rock. He checked the readings, readjusted the scope's focus, and confirmed that this particular dune was devoid of any laborers or soldiers. It had completely escaped Belloq's attention.

Indy stood up behind the transit and gazed at the unexcavated dune. He smiled and said, "That's it."

Belloq practically had to push his way through the thick atmosphere of dust that drifted over the excavation site. Leading Dietrich and Gobler past the many men who were hard at work digging or carrying dirt away in baskets and carts, Belloq said, "Who knows? Perhaps the Ark is still waiting in some antechamber for us to discover."

Neither Belloq nor the Germans noticed Sallah walk by. Following Indy's instructions, Sallah had set off to round up a group of trustworthy diggers. Sallah heard Belloq's comment, and struggled to suppress a smug grin as he moved on, away from the other men.

"Perhaps," Belloq continued, "there's some vital bit of evidence which eludes us." Pausing to gaze at the workers, he said, "Perhaps —"

"Perhaps the girl can help us," Gobler interrupted, referring to Marion.

"My feeling exactly," Dietrich said as Belloq turned with an annoyed scowl. Dietrich continued, "She was in possession of the original piece for years. She may know much if properly motivated."

Keeping his eyes fixed on Dietrich, Belloq said evenly, "I tell you, the girl knows nothing."

Dietrich chuckled. "I'm surprised to find you squeamish. That is not your reputation. But it needn't concern you." Turning away from Belloq, Dietrich looked to an approaching figure as he added, "I have the perfect man for this kind of work."

Belloq followed Dietrich's gaze. Through the rising dust, he saw a man walking toward them. The man wore a black hat, suit, and heavy leather trench coat. Belloq imagined the man must be impossibly hot in such clothes. The man wended neatly around the many diggers until he arrived before Belloq and the two German officers.

And then Arnold Toht, peering at the men through his wire-frame glasses, raised his right hand and said, "Heil Hitler."

Belloq winced at the sight of the dark-suited man's open palm. It displayed a hideous scar, a souvenir from the red-hot headpiece to the Staff of Ra that Toht had momentarily clutched in Nepal. The headpiece had seared Toht's flesh, leaving an imprint from which the Nazis were able to make a mold, and from that mold construct a replica of the headpiece. Although the replica — like the scar — showed only one side of the original headpiece, it had enabled Belloq to enter the map room in Tanis and pinpoint the location of the Well of Souls. Or so Belloq had thought.

Toht smiled at Belloq. As much as Belloq wanted to find the Well of Souls and the Ark of the Covenant, he didn't like the idea of unleashing Toht on Marion Ravenwood.

Indy and Sallah led ten men, all carrying shovels and picks, away from the main excavation. They walked past the dunes to arrive beside the one that Indy had surveyed earlier. While Sallah and his crew waited below, Indy scrambled up the dune to stand at the top and scan the area. He was literally a stone's throw from several diggers near the base of the dune, and in plain sight of many more laborers and soldiers stationed on and around the dune where Belloq believed they would find the Ark. With so many hundreds of people at work and all the rising dust, Indy — who was still wearing his robes and *keffiyeh* — didn't draw any attention whatsoever. He felt like the proverbial needle in a haystack.

Turning away from his view of Belloq's dig, Indy held his fingers to his lips and released a sharp, quick whistle. His signal brought Sallah and his crew up to the top of the dune. As a precaution against inquiring soldiers, they positioned a tripod-mounted transit and some other surveying equipment at the upper edge of the dune, which served to make their operation appear to be official, should any soldiers question them.

Sallah and the ten men watched as Indy plunged his own shovel into the dune's sandy surface, and then they did the same. Despite his concerns about Marion's safety and the risk of being discovered by the Germans, Indy couldn't help but be excited — he was so close to making the archaeological discovery of the century. He didn't just *think* that the Well of Souls was directly under their feet. He was certain of it.

They worked all the rest of that day without incident. Progress was slow but steady, and the men sometimes sang as they shoveled and chipped away at the top of the dune. The nearby soldiers never gave them a second glance.

The sun was setting and the winds were picking up when Indy looked away from his dune to see that most of the soldiers were returning to their camp for the night. Emboldened by the approaching darkness, he removed his *keffiyeh* and robes. He had been wearing his own clothes underneath the robes all day, and it felt good to air out. Then he put on his fedora, and he felt even better.

As darkness fell, Sallah's crew set up a few low torches around their work area so that they could keep working through the night. But as the hours passed, and the winds became stronger and ominous clouds appeared over the desert, some of the workers grew uneasy with their task. A few began muttering prayers.

Indy looked away from the dune and saw a sudden flash of lightning in the distance. When another series of bolts rippled across the sky, even he began to reconsider whether they should continue the dig. His apprehension had nothing to with superstition. Any former Boy Scout knew it was downright dangerous to be out in the open during a lightning storm. But the excitement of being so close to finding the Ark overwhelmed any thoughts of safety.

Sallah called out, "Indy! Here! We've hit stone!"

Indy ran over to Sallah, kneeled down on the ground beside him, and began pushing the sand back with his fingers. Under the sand, Indy felt the smooth, hard surface of cut stone. "Clear it off!" he ordered the crew. "Come on, find the edges!"

All the men dropped to their knees and began pushing the sand back, searching for the edges of the stone slab. Seconds later, they found the narrow grooves that revealed the slab was a large, expertly cut rectangle.

"Good, good, good!" Sallah said when he saw the full rectangle revealed. "You see, Indy? You see?"

Overhead, thunder rumbled. Indy was now oblivious to the noise. "Okay," he said, "bring the pry bars in!"

Flashes of lightning illuminated the dune as the men grabbed their long metal pry bars and wedged them down into the groove around the slab. Sallah shouted, "As a team, boys! As a team!"

When Indy saw that all the men were ready, he yelled, "Push!"

The men pressed against their pry bars. Sallah felt the muscles in his arms and legs straining, but then he heard the satisfying sound of grinding stone as the great slab began to shift.

"Get 'em in there," Indy urged the men with the pry bars. "Get 'em under." As the slab began to lift from its recessed position, he continued, "Good, good, that's it. Watch your toes!"

The winds became fiercer. As the slab lifted higher, a jet of dusty air blasted out from underneath it. A moment later, the slab lay at an angle across a dark, rectangular opening. Sallah directed his men to lay down their pry bars so they could grab the edges of the slab with their hands and lift it aside. As they moved the slab away from the opening, Sallah gasped, "Carefully! Carefully!"

When the opening was fully exposed, Sallah grabbed a torch and kneeled down beside Indy to look down into a deep, dark chamber. Before their eyes could adjust to the darkness, lightning flashed, and both men found themselves looking into the eyes and gaping maw of a monstrous head.

Sallah screamed and recoiled. Indy didn't flinch.

He saw the monstrous head for what it was: the top of an enormous statue of Anubis, the Egyptian god of the dead, who had a human body and a jackal's head.

Recovering himself, Sallah said, "Sorry, Indy." He adjusted the angle of his torch and looked down again. The chamber below appeared to be about thirty feet deep. The enormous statue of Anubis was one of four, all of which faced toward the center of the ceiling and stood with their arms raised to support the roof. At the far end of the chamber, there was a stone altar, an elaborately carved platform on which rested a large stone chest covered with Egyptian hieroglyphics. The chamber's floor was covered by some kind of dark carpet, and after studying it for a moment, Sallah said, "Indy . . . why does the floor move?"

"Give me your torch," Indy said.

Sallah handed Indy the torch, and Indy dropped it into the chamber. As the torch landed on the floor, the area around it erupted into a sudden chorus of hisses and slithering sounds.

The entire floor was blanketed with thousands of snakes.

Indy slowly rolled his body away from the edge of the opening. "Snakes," he muttered. "Why'd it have to be snakes?"

Sallah studied the distant snakes. "Asps," he observed. "Very dangerous." Looking to Indy, he said encouragingly, "*You* go first."

CHAPTER TWELVE

Still bound, gagged, and seated on the sandy ground under the striped tent, Marion had fallen asleep against the tent's central support pole. But when she felt someone's hands against the back of her neck, she awoke with a start and let out a muffled scream.

The hands behind Marion belonged to Belloq, who had crouched down to untie the gag and ropes. Marion glanced from Belloq to another man in the tent, an attendant, who had just placed a tray of food and a pitcher of water on a nearby table. As Belloq stood up and tossed the gag onto another small table, Marion — too sore to stand up right away — wriggled away from the pole and crawled fast toward the tent's open flap. She got only as far as the edge of the tent when a tall German guard suddenly appeared in front of her, blocking her exit. The guard held a rifle.

"If you're trying to escape on foot," Belloq said casually, "the desert is three weeks in every direction." He gestured to the food on the table and said, "So please, eat something."

Still on her knees, Marion glanced from Belloq to the guard, and then turned and crawled back into the tent, heading for the table. As she crawled, the attendant walked past the guard and exited the tent. When Marion arrived beside the table, she quickly brushed the sand from her hands, then picked up a piece of bread and began gobbling it up.

Belloq said, "I must apologize for their treatment of you."

With her mouth full of food, Marion said, "Yeah? Whose idea was it? No food, no water. What kind of people are these friends of yours?"

"At this particular time and place, to do my work, they are necessary evils. They're not my friends." Belloq turned to pick up a cardboard box, placing it on his lap as he sat down in a chair across from Marion. "However," he continued, "with the right connections, even in this part of the world, we are not entirely uncivilized."

Belloq reached into the cardboard box and held up a delicate white dress. Marion, still working on the food, gave the dress a dismissive glance, but shrugged and said, "It's beautiful."

Staring into Marion's eyes, Belloq said, "I would very much like to see you in it."

"Ha!" Marion laughed. "I'll bet you would." But then she seemed to soften slightly under Belloq's gaze, as if she were reconsidering her situation. Tossing an uneaten bit of food onto the tray, she stood up and said, "All right." She reached for the dress and practically yanked it out of the box. As she held the dress up against her body to see that it looked like it would be a perfect fit, Belloq reached into the bottom of the box and pulled out a pair of matching high-heeled shoes, which he handed to her.

Marion took the shoes. As she turned and carried the dress and shoes behind a tall screen, she said, "What do you got to drink around here?"

Belloq set the empty box on the floor and rose from his chair. "We don't have much time," he said as he stepped over to a bureau where he kept his cologne. The bureau had a small round mirror on top of it, and Belloq dabbed his neck and jawline with cologne. He removed a bottle from a bureau drawer and said, "Soon they will come to harm you, and I will not be able to stop them, unless you are able to give me something to placate them. Some, uh, piece of information . . . which I can use to protect you from them."

"I've already told you everything I know," Marion said from behind the screen. "I have no loyalty to Jones. He's brought me nothing but trouble."

When Marion emerged from behind the screen, she smiled at Belloq. The dress was made of silk and satin, very expensive, and was decorated with fabric roses. Like the dress, the shoes also fit perfectly. If Marion felt any discomfort walking across the sandy floor in high heels, her radiant smile didn't betray her, and she even managed a fashion model-like turn.

"Marion," Belloq said smoothly, "you are beautiful."

Belloq didn't seem to notice that Marion was clutching her old clothes. As she moved back to the dining table, she tossed the clothes down on the edge of the table, beside her plate, to conceal the silver-plated knife that she'd placed there only a minute earlier. She had taken the knife from the tray of food when Belloq had turned to pick up the box that contained the dress, and she wanted it within reach when she was ready to make her move.

Keeping her eyes and smile on Belloq, she picked up the bottle he'd placed on the table and said, "I don't think we need a chaperone."

Belloq made a sweeping hand gesture to the guard stationed at the tent's exit. The guard stepped away from the tent, leaving Marion alone with Belloq.

Clinging to a long rope, Indy dangled in the air above the snake-covered floor of the Well of Souls. Above him, Sallah guided the other men to lower Indy slowly. Sallah had made good on his promise to replace Indy's Smith & Wesson Hand Ejector, Model 2, but Indy took little comfort in the gun that now rested in the holster at his right hip. As grateful as he was to Sallah, the revolver would be about as useful against thousands of snakes as a peashooter in a lion's den.

"Steadily ... steadily ..." Sallah urged his crew, but then the rope began to slip and Indy suddenly dropped a few feet. "Whoa!" Sallah yelled.

Indy's grip tightened on the rope as he came to a jerking stop in front of the nearest jackal-headed statue. Looking below, he saw that the statue was poised with its left leg forward, and that he would have to descend carefully or he'd bump into its skirt. He planted the soles of his boots on the jackal's carved teeth, and then kicked out to clear the statue's torso as the crew above resumed lowering him.

"Down ..." Sallah ordered. "Down — whoa. Carefully, carefully!" Sallah looked below to see that Indy was about halfway down now, swinging slightly back and forth in the space between the statues. "You all right, Indy?"

Indy gave no reply as his eyes scanned the ground below. He had tossed down fifteen torches in advance, which served to illuminate the chamber's interior and also created a clear zone, as they drove back the snakes from the small area directly below the opening in the ceiling. However, the torches also illuminated the legions of snakes throughout the rest of chamber. The sight of this subterranean landscape of slithering forms, bared fangs, and snapping jaws left Indy mute with fear.

"Now gently, boys," Sallah's voice echoed down from the opening. "Gently, gently!"

Without warning, the crew lost their purchase on the sandy roof, causing Indy to fall the few remaining feet. He grunted as he landed on his side and rolled onto his stomach, and when he lifted his head, he was face-to-face with a large cobra.

The cobra's head was raised, poised to strike. Indy just gaped at it. Behind him, the rope swung back and forth, brushing against the backs of his extended legs.

Sallah peered down through the opening and saw Indy's form at the edge of the clear zone. Unaware of Indy's proximity to the cobra, Sallah smiled and shouted down, "I told you it would be all right!"

Indy's lower lip trembled. He wanted to tell Sallah to be quiet but was so afraid that he could barely breathe.

The cobra hissed, and then its head swayed slightly, bobbing in front of Indy like a deadly, hypnotic pendulum. Indy kept his eyes fixed on the cobra as he slowly pushed himself away, inch by inch.

When he was a full four feet away from the cobra, Indy tried to get himself under control. He felt nerveless and completely exposed to the snakes. Then he remembered the supplies that he had already lowered into the chamber: a metal bucket, a small pump with an attached hose, and a cylindrical can of gasoline. He focused on these objects and tried to ignore the snakes. It wasn't easy.

Rising from the floor, Indy kicked at the sand to drive back some nearby snakes. As he lifted the can of gasoline, he looked up to the opening at the ceiling. In a shaky voice, he shouted, "Sallah, get down here!" Then he turned and poured the gasoline into the bucket.

While Sallah prepared his own descent, Indy placed the pump into the bucket. He held the end of the hose with one hand as he worked the pump with the other, spraying gasoline onto the snakes that were between him and the chamber's altar. Some snakes hissed and moved away as the spray met their bodies, but most just continued to wriggle and slither around the perimeter of the clear zone.

Lousy snakes, Indy thought. After he'd sprayed a good amount of gasoline, he lowered the hose and pump, stepped away from the bucket, and picked up a blazing torch. Then he tossed the torch at the gasoline-covered snakes. There was a loud *foom!* as the gas ignited and created a wall of flame.

* * *

Seated across the small dining table from Belloq in the tent, Marion eyed the bottle that stood beside their empty glasses. Wearing her most alluring smile, she said, "You pour."

Belloq removed the bottle's cork and poured a small amount into each glass. He bowed his head slightly and smiled at Marion as they raised their glasses and clinked them together, and then he took a small sip from his glass.

Marion lifted her eyebrows playfully, and then tossed her drink down in one gulp. Seeing this, Belloq's eyes went wide with surprise. Marion maintained her smile as she gazed challengingly at Belloq.

Belloq looked at the remaining contents of his own glass, then tossed his down in the same manner. A moment later, he let out a sharp, dry cough.

Marion grinned as she refilled their glasses.

With Sallah now by his side in the Well of Souls, Indy carried a torch as they walked slowly over the snake-free path they had cleared to reach the altar. A short flight of stone steps led up to the top of the ornate platform that supported the hieroglyphic-covered stone chest. Taking a moment to study the hieroglyphics, Indy confirmed that the Egyptian pharaoh Shishak had commissioned the Well of Souls to contain the Ark of the Covenant, just as the legends had told.

After climbing the steps, Indy placed his gloved hands on the surface of the thick slab of stone that was the chest's lid. A thin layer of sand covered the lid, and Indy brushed it aside to see that the lid was free of ornamentation. It appeared that the snakes had never nested on or around the platform and chest. Indy could only imagine why.

He reached to the outer, lower edge of the lid to find his grip, and then motioned to Sallah to move to the other side of the chest. Gripping the lid at the same time, they bent their knees and pushed up. The lid outweighed Indy and Sallah combined, and both men clenched their teeth as their muscles tensed and the slab began to rise. Seconds later, they'd lifted the lid clear of the chest, but with no one else to help them, they had few options for where to place it.

Indy and Sallah let go of the stone lid. It cracked and crumbled as it tumbled down the platform's steps.

Even though the lid had been undecorated, it also had been an archaeological treasure, as was every other artifact within the Well of Souls. But Indy had to live with the fact that he didn't have the time or the resources to stop the Nazis from eventually finding and seizing the ruined lid, the hieroglyphs, the towering statues, or anything else that they would claim after his work here was done. The only thing that mattered was his objective, which was now fully revealed to him as he and Sallah peered into the open stone chest to see the Ark of the Covenant.

The Ark gleamed. Although its box-shaped body was made of acacia wood, it was overlaid with gold. Its top was adorned with an elaborate gold crown, and two golden, winged cherubs who faced each other with bowed heads. Indy estimated the Ark was about four feet long, two and a half feet wide, and two and a half feet high. When he noticed the gold carrying rings that were attached to each corner, he realized it was time to stop staring at the Ark, and time to start getting the Ark out of the Well of Souls and into Sallah's waiting truck.

Sallah's crew had already finished building a makeshift winch to hoist the Ark out. Indy hoped to cover their trail, but he imagined the Nazis would find the

Well of Souls within the next day or so. If all went well, the Ark of the Covenant would be long gone by then.

However, Indy had another problem: Marion. He had no intention of leaving her behind, but hadn't figured out a way to rescue her either. Right now, all he could do was hope that she was safe.

Marion and Belloq were both laughing in the tent. Marion laughed so hard she fell out of her chair.

"Whoops," Belloq said, and then they were both off laughing again.

Now seated on the ground beside the table, Marion reached up for her glass and quickly drained it. She laughed some more as she reached for the nearly emptied bottle, studied its label, and said, "What is this stuff, René?"

Taking the bottle and holding it proudly, Belloq chortled, "I grew up with this. It's my family label."

This made Marion laugh even harder. She took the bottle back from him and tried to pour some more into her glass, but she missed. Belloq found this quite amusing, laughing as he took the bottle back from her and filled her glass himself. This made them both laugh, too. But when Belloq put the bottle down, Marion stopped laughing and made her move.

Her hand darted out for the knife that she'd concealed earlier. Snatching the knife by its handle, she brought it back in front of her, the tip of its blade angled at Belloq. She was still on the ground, and all she had to do was spring forward to drive the blade into his chest.

Belloq's smile fell as he looked from Marion's blazing eyes to the knife in her grip. And then, because he knew she had no serious chance of escaping, he burst out laughing again.

Playing along as she had been the whole time they'd been in the tent, Marion laughed, too. "Well . . ." she said through the laughter, "I have to be going now, René." As she backed away toward the open tent flaps, she added, "I like you, René, very much. Perhaps we'll meet someday under better circumstances."

Marion was still backing up when she bumped into someone behind her. She whirled fast with the knife, but the man who had just entered the tent caught her wrist in his black-gloved hand.

It was Arnold Toht. His leather trench coat was draped over his back like a black cape, which somehow heightened his nightmarish appearance.

Marion's eyes went wide. Toht said, "We meet again, Fräulein."

Recovering fast, Marion tried to stab the fiend, but he held tight to her wrist. "You Americans, you're all the same," Toht said as he increased his pressure on her wrist, forcing her fingers to open and drop the knife, which fell to the sandy floor. "Always overdressing for the wrong occasions."

Marion broke free from Toht's grasp and ran back to Belloq, who had remained seated at the table. Marion huddled beside Belloq as she returned her gaze to Toht.

Dietrich and Gobler entered the tent. Gobler carried a black leather bag, which he handed to Toht before he took Toht's trench coat.

Toht reached into his bag and removed a set of three black metal rods, which were linked together by thin steel chains. Toht held the rods out before him, then gave them a slight jerk that produced a sudden snap as the connecting chains went taut. Belloq's body tensed in response to the noise, and Marion gasped in horror as she imagined what Toht would do next.

Then Toht made an adjustment to the device, flipping one rod over the other to transform it into a coat hanger. He held it out to Gobler, who placed Toht's coat on it before he took the hanger and coat back.

Both Marion and Belloq breathed a sigh of relief.

Toht moved away from Gobler and Dietrich, and then sat down in the chair that Marion had previously occupied. Facing Marion, who now cringed behind Belloq, Toht leered and said, "Now . . . what shall we talk about?"

CHAPTER THIRTEEN

*I*t was dawn when Indy and Sallah slid two long, wooden poles through the Ark's gold carrying rings. Standing on opposite sides of the exposed stone chest, they slowly raised the poles, lifted the Ark out, and proceeded to carry it carefully across the floor of the Well of Souls.

A few of the torches that lay on the floor had already gone out. Indy noticed that the snakes seemed to be getting restless. He could only imagine whether they were anxious about the morning sky, which could be glimpsed through the ceiling's rectangular opening, or the Ark's imminent departure from their dark lair, but he would be glad to put all the snakes behind him.

When Indy and Sallah reached the area directly below the ceiling's opening, they lowered the Ark into a wooden crate that Sallah's crew had sent down by ropes earlier. After they secured the crate and made sure the ropes would hold, Indy picked up a torch and signaled to the crew above. "All right!" he said. "Take it up!"

The crated Ark began to rise away from Indy and Sallah. Holding the torch with one hand, Indy kept his other hand on the side of the crate, steadying it, until it lifted above his head. "Easy!" he said.

A snake hissed near Indy's feet. He swung the torch over the snakes, driving the snake back. He knew it would take just a couple of minutes for the crew to hoist the crate out through the opening, and then he and Sallah could make their exit, too. As more snakes started to slither toward him and Sallah, Indy found himself wishing the crew would move just a bit faster.

The sun had just begun to rise over the desert when Colonel Dietrich and Toht followed Belloq out of the tent where they'd left Marion, who hadn't told them anything that they didn't know already. As the three men walked across the compound, passing the slumbering forms of Arab laborers who had been forced to sleep wherever they could under the open sky, Dietrich jutted his square jaw at Belloq and sniped, "You're as stubborn as that girl."

Toht giggled and added, "You like her too much, I think."

Ignoring Toht, Belloq glanced at Dietrich and said,

"Your methods of archaeology are too primitive for me. You would use a bulldozer to find a . . . china cup."

Distracted by something he saw off to his right, Belloq slowed, and then came to a complete stop. The other two men stopped, too, and then watched Belloq as he ran over to a nearby wooden ramp and jumped up on it for an elevated view. Following Belloq's gaze, Dietrich and Toht saw what he was looking at: A group of laborers, silhouetted against the dawn sky, were already at work on top of a nearby dune, and it appeared they had utilized a few long poles to construct a rudimentary winch. The silhouette of a large box rested near the winch.

Turning to Dietrich, Belloq shouted, "Colonel! Wake your men!"

Keeping close to the rope that dangled down into the Well of Souls, Indy and Sallah watched each other's backs while the snakes slithered toward them. They held their torches low and waved them back and forth to keep the snakes at bay. Glancing at the other torches that they'd placed around the clear zone, Sallah commented, "Indy, the torches are burning out."

Indy reached for Sallah's torch and took it, so he was now holding one in each hand. "Go on," he said, "get out of here."

Sallah turned for the rope. While he began climbing up, Indy swung and jabbed the two torches at the nearest snakes. When Sallah was about halfway to the opening, Indy realized the torch in his left hand was about to fizzle out. He held tight to the torch in his right hand as he dropped the other, leaving his left hand free to grab the rope.

Neither Sallah nor Indy heard the rifle-toting German soldiers who came running up the dune above their heads. Just a moment after Sallah clambered out through the ceiling, the entire length of rope slipped down through the opening. Seeing the rope land in a heap near his feet, Indy raised his head to the ceiling as he yelled, "Sallah!"

"Hello!" a voice called from above. It wasn't Sallah who looked down at Indy from the high, rectangular opening. It was Belloq.

"Hello," Belloq repeated as he held his Panama hat and waved it at Indy. "Why, Dr. Jones, whatever are you doing in such a nasty place?"

Despite a momentary shock, Indy shouted back, "Why don't you come down here? I'll *show* you!"

"Thank you, my friend," Belloq said, kneeling at the edge of the opening, "but I think we are all very comfortable up here." Belloq looked away, and then said, "That's right, isn't it?"

From below, Indy saw two German officers step up beside Belloq. Indy guessed one of the officers was Dietrich, the ringleader that Sallah had told him about. He hadn't heard any shots fired, so Indy hoped Sallah was all right. He backed up slightly, and saw that the Ark was right behind Belloq. He also saw more soldiers.

Returning his gaze to Indy, Belloq continued, "Yes, we are very comfortable up here. So, once again, Jones, what was briefly yours is now mine. What a fitting end to your life's pursuits. You're about to become a permanent addition to this archaeological find. Who knows? In a thousand years, even you may be worth something."

Rattled and infuriated as Indy was, he responded with bravado. He smiled broadly, and then laughed before muttering a curse under his breath. A sudden hissing to his right prompted him to look away from Belloq for a moment as he swung his torch at some more snakes.

"I'm afraid we must be going now, Dr. Jones," Dietrich said casually. "Our prize is awaited in Berlin. But we do not wish to leave you down in that awful place all alone."

Hearing this, Belloq appeared baffled and concerned as he glanced at Dietrich. Before Belloq could say anything, he saw Toht and Marion approach from behind the armed soldiers who had encircled the top of the dune and captured Sallah and his crew. Marion was still in the white dress and shoes that Belloq had given her, and Toht gripped her arms tightly from behind. As Toht pushed her past the soldiers, Marion shouted, "Slimy pig, you let me go! Stop it!"

And then Toht shoved Marion straight toward the rectangular opening.

"No!" Belloq shouted as she tumbled forward and screamed.

Though the soldiers had their rifles leveled at Sallah, he bravely lunged for Marion, but his outstretched hands met empty air. Fortunately, Marion's own hands caught something else.

"Marion!" Indy shouted as a white, high-heeled shoe landed in a tangle of snakes. He looked up to see Marion clinging to the carved teeth in the lower jaw of one of the Anubis statues. Her right shoe was still on, and her bare legs kicked at the air below her shimmering white dress. Indy had already dropped his torch and he ignored the snakes as he held out his arms and moved below Marion's dangling body. "Hang on! Don't —"

"Indy!" Marion cried. The statue's teeth had not been constructed to support weight, and the tooth that she gripped in her right hand began to crumble.

"Don't fall!" Indy shouted. "Marion! I got you!"

The statue's tooth broke away from its jaw and Marion screamed again as she fell. The carved skirt that jutted out over the statue's slightly extended knee broke her fall, and she landed in Indy's waiting arms. He gasped and his knees buckled as he caught her, then they both collapsed to the ground.

"You traitor!" Marion shouted as she twisted against Indy's leather jacket and pushed herself free from his arms. "You get your hands off of me!" She rolled away from him, landed on her stomach, and lifted her head at the same moment that another creature raised its own to face her. It was only then that Marion realized that she and Indy weren't alone in the chamber.

Marion had landed beside several dozen snakes, and a cobra's elevated head was only an arm's length away. Marion stared at the cobra with wide-eyed fear and pulled away fast. The cobra snapped at her, but missed. Marion yelled as she scrambled back to Indy and jumped on top of him, clinging to his back as he struggled to stand.

"Snakes!" Marion gasped as she wriggled to straddle Indy's back. "Oh. Oh, at your feet!"

Indy sidestepped another group of snakes as he tried to keep his balance, which wasn't easy. The way Marion was climbing him, she seemed to have forgotten that he was a man and not a tree.

Belloq had seen Marion's landing from the edge of the opening above, but now shifted his gaze to Dietrich. With obvious outrage, Belloq said, "The girl was mine!"

"She's of no use to us," Dietrich replied sharply as he stepped beside the crate that contained the Ark. "Only our mission for the Führer matters. I wonder sometimes, monsieur, if you have that clearly in mind."

As Dietrich left to prepare his report to Berlin, Belloq gazed back down through the opening. He saw Marion sitting in Indy's arms, with her own arms wrapped around his neck. Sounding somewhat regretful, Belloq called down, "It was not to be, chérie!"

Now cradling Marion in his arms, Indy turned so that they could both look up and face Belloq. "You rats!" Marion shouted back. "I'll get you for this!"

Belloq said, "Indiana Jones . . . adieu." He gave a slight wave with his Panama hat, and then stepped aside as the German soldiers forced Sallah's crew to lift the stone slab that lay at the edge of the opening.

Sallah watched helplessly as his men began to slide the stone slab back over the opening. The only person who was actually enjoying the situation was Toht, who leered and began to giggle as he walked off after Dietrich.

Staring at the diminishing rectangle of daylight above her, Marion screamed, "Nooooo — !" Her long cry was cut off to the outside world as the slab fell into place, leaving her and Indy trapped within the Well of Souls.

CHAPTER FOURTEEN

*I*ndy put Marion down on the ground beside him, where she stood awkwardly in her one high-heeled shoe. As the snakes began to move in, Indy snatched up the two torches that appeared to have the most life left in them. Handing one of the torches to Marion, he said, "Take this. Wave it at anything that slithers."

"Thank you," Marion gasped as she seized the torch. Sweeping the torch over some nearby snakes, she muttered, "This whole place is slitherin'."

Indy stepped a short distance away from Marion to wave his own torch at some other snakes. As he moved, Marion saw a serpentine shape shift against Indy's left hip. "Indy!" she shouted as she quickly jabbed her torch at Indy's leg.

"Ow!" Indy yelled as he jerked away from the flames. Glaring at Marion, he turned his body so she could plainly see that she had mistaken his coiled whip for a snake.

If it occurred to Marion that she should apologize, that thought vanished as more snakes slid toward them. As she returned her attention to the snake, Indy leaned in close beside her and tugged at the sleeve of her white dress. "Where did you get this?" he said in an accusing tone. "From him?"

"I was trying to escape!" Marion snapped back. "No thanks to you."

"How hard were you trying?" Indy said as he kicked sand at some snakes.

"Well, where were you? You —"

"Watch it, watch it," Indy interrupted, motioning to Marion to keep her torch away from him. Without explanation, he dropped to one knee beside Marion, grabbed the hem of her dress and began tearing at it.

"What are you doing?!" Marion screamed as the lower half of the dress ripped free from around her legs.

"For the fire!" Indy shouted, as if his answer was obvious. He wrapped the fabric around his torch.

Knowing that a few strips of fabric wasn't going to keep them alive indefinitely, Marion said, "How are we going to get out of here?"

"I'm working on it! I'm working on it!"

"Well, whatever you're doin', do it faster!"

Indy saw movement against a nearby wall that was covered with hieroglyphics. Snakes were slithering in through cracks and holes that had formed in the wall over the centuries. Seeing the way the snakes were entering the Well of Souls, Indy realized there must be another chamber on the other side of the wall.

"Ah . . ." he said with a smile as he turned away from the wall and stepped over to the base of one of the towering statues.

Seeing Indy's movement, Marion said, "Where are you goin'?"

"Through that wall," Indy said, pointing to the wall where snakes continued to spill out from the cracks and holes. "Just get ready to run, whatever happens to me."

"What do you mean by that?" Marion asked as she waved her torch at some snakes. But when she glanced back at Indy, he was already clambering up the legs of the jackal-headed statue.

Although Indy's torch was dying, it was still burning enough to help him see the statue in the darkness. To keep both of his hands free, he placed the torch in his mouth, biting down on its grip so that the burning end was well away from his face. After he shimmied up over the statue's knee, he reached for his whip. Indy drew back his arm, then flung the whip up so that its end wrapped tightly around the statue's lower jaw. Then he tugged at the taut whip to make sure it would hold, and began scaling the statue's torso.

"Indy!" Marion shouted from below. "Don't you leave me down here by myself!"

Still holding his torch between his clenched teeth, Indy was lifting himself up past the statue's open mouth when he saw a coiled snake nestled between the statue's long, sculpted teeth, just inches from his face. The snake gazed back at him as its tongue darted out of its mouth. Unable to use his hands without losing his grip, Indy turned his head quickly to swing his torch's burning end directly into the snake.

The snake emitted a screaming hiss as it jerked away from the flames and tumbled out of the statue's mouth. The snake's body landed on Marion's shoulders. Marion screamed and shook the snake off and threw an angered glare at Indy.

With some dismay, Indy saw that his torch was now extinguished. Seeing Marion looking up at him, he opened his mouth and let the torch fall. Marion caught the torch's grip in her free hand, and then began swinging both torches at the snakes, using the extinguished torch like a club.

Indy quickly found his footing, removed his whip from the statue's jaw, and climbed up onto the back of the statue's head. Bracing his own arms and back against the ceiling, he pushed out against the statue with his legs. The ancient statue shifted slightly, and dust came raining down from its body. Indy grimaced with exertion as he continued to push. More dust rained down and there was a crumbling sound as the statue began to break loose from the ceiling.

"Indy!" Marion yelled as the statue started to sway under Indy's strain. The snakes were all around her now.

"Here we go!" Indy shouted from atop the statue. "Get ready!"

"Indy, the torch is going out!"

The statue's left forearm snapped in half and the entire figure began to topple. Indy wrapped his whip around the statue's shattered left arm as he jumped down from its head, neatly tucking his body against the statue so he could ride it as it fell. Just as he'd planned, the statue smashed hard into — and through — the targeted wall.

Marion had narrowly missed being struck by the falling statue, and lost sight of Indy amidst the crumbling stones and flying dust. But when she saw that the crash had created an opening in the wall that led to another chamber, she scrambled over the rubble, moving carefully to avoid any snakes. When she realized that she was holding her remaining high-heel shoe in one hand, she tossed the useless thing aside and continued on barefoot.

As she moved into the dark, adjoining chamber, her hands touched upon an object and she gripped it to steady her balance. She said, "Indy?"

She didn't know that her hands were on a decrepit mummy until it tumbled from its resting place and into her arms. Marion screamed as she shoved the mummy aside and backed away from it. Unfortunately, she backed straight into another mummy. She yelled again, but her next move revealed that foul-smelling mummies were everywhere, with their bony arms extended and waiting to snatch at her. As she shrieked and stumbled through the catacombs, she saw a large snake slither through the remains of a human skull, and she screamed even louder.

"Marion!" Indy shouted as he pushed his way through the catacombs. His hat and jacket were covered in dust, but he was uninjured. Finding Marion had been a breeze. He had just followed her screams. Taking her by the arm, he said, "Look. Look." He pushed through some cobwebs and led her into a narrow, stone-walled chamber. At the end of the chamber, just beyond the rubble-covered floor, sunlight peeked through between the blocks of stones in the wall.

Indy knew an exit when he saw one. While Marion got her breath back, he stepped over the rubble and began pushing against the blocks until he found a loose one. Pressing his weight against it, he shoved it until it budged some more, and then kept pushing until he sent it clear out of the wall. Indy slumped over the newly opened space while the heavy block landed with a loud thud on the ground outside.

Looking ragged and covered with dirt, Marion came up behind Indy and followed him through the opening. They had emerged outside some weathered ruins overlooking an area that the Germans had set up as an airfield bordered by a few small buildings and a spindly-looking watchtower. Several soldiers, a few military vehicles, and a gasoline tanker were visible, along with a single aircraft: a strange-looking plane that was essentially a large fixed wing without a fuselage or tail section.

At the front of the plane, there was a cockpit with a glass canopy that offered the pilot maximum visibility. Opposite the cockpit, a glass-domed gun turret was positioned at the aft area of the wing between two large propellers. The plane was adorned with Nazi swastikas. Indy had heard that the Nazis had been working on the development of such a "flying wing" configuration, but had no idea that any had gone into production. For all he knew, this one was a prototype.

The Flying Wing's engine was already running and its propellers spinning as Indy and Marion snuck away from the ruins to hide behind some barrels near the airfield. From this position, they watched the pilot raise the cockpit canopy, allowing the pilot to stand upright while he checked the controls. As a light-armored car sped away from the airfield, Indy realized what the Germans were preparing to do with the Ark. "They're gonna fly it out of here," he said. Thinking quickly, he added, "When that Ark gets loaded, we're already gonna be on the plane."

Because the Germans finally possessed the Ark of the Covenant, the laborers were informed that their work was done. They gathered around the perimeter of the camp, waiting to be paid and watching the armed soldiers warily.

Belloq stepped out of the German Command Tent to find Colonel Dietrich seated in a chair, his boots resting on an adjacent table. A short distance away rested the wooden crate that contained the Ark. A soldier was busily stenciling the words *EIGENTUM DER DEUTSCHEN WEHRMACHT*, and a Nazi emblem onto the crate, just in time for the arrival of the light-armored car that had traveled from the nearby airfield.

Dietrich had already sent his radio message to Berlin, notifying his superiors about his acquisition of the Ark, and as he poured a glass of cognac, he looked very pleased with himself. Seeing Belloq step up beside him,

Dietrich said, "Ah, monsieur. Let us toast our success in the desert." He held out the glass to Belloq and said, "To the Ark."

Ignoring the offered glass, Belloq replied petulantly, "When we are *very* far from here. That will do." He stepped over the crate to inspect it before it was loaded into the waiting car.

While Marion remained concealed behind the barrels, Indy trotted out from their hiding space and dashed toward the Flying Wing. The pilot was still in the cockpit, but was so focused on checking and adjusting the plane's instruments that he didn't see Indy dart under the plane. Indy kept a careful distance from the plane's rotating propellers, but was relieved that the engines were already running. They were so loud that he didn't even have to run quietly.

The pilot had left the cockpit canopy open, leaving him exposed from behind. Indy planned on sneaking up from the back of the plane, but as he climbed onto the aft section of the wide wing and began to crawl toward the cockpit, he suddenly heard someone shouting over the noise of the engines. Turning his head, he saw a German mechanic standing just behind the plane. *Uh-oh.*

CHAPTER FIFTEEN

*T*he mechanic was about Indy's size, and wore a green T-shirt and khaki pants. Indy knew the man must be a mechanic because he was holding an extremely large wrench. Indy lifted his own hands to show they were empty, and turned slowly toward the mechanic. Feinting that he was about to step down from the back of the plane, Indy suddenly kicked the mechanic in the jaw.

The mechanic fell backwards, but held tight to his wrench as he rolled to the ground. Although Indy was carrying a gun, he didn't want to shoot the mechanic — gunfire might alert the pilot and other soldiers. Indy leaped after the fallen mechanic, but the mechanic sprang to his feet and swung his wrench at Indy.

Indy dodged the swing and launched his fist into the mechanic's jaw, knocking him to the ground again. The tough mechanic jumped up and resumed his attack with the wrench, swinging at Indy and forcing his opponent back toward one of the spinning propellers.

Neither man noticed Marion had snuck below the Flying Wing to crouch down beside the landing gear. They were also unaware that their fight had attracted the attention of another German soldier: a bald, hulking brute who had just emerged from a nearby building. The bald man enjoyed boxing, and wasn't about to let one of his fellow soldiers get beaten up by some scruffy-looking interloper. Eager to join in the fight, he began removing his shirt as he walked slowly toward Indy and the mechanic.

Indy grabbed the mechanic and pushed his arm toward the propeller. There was a bright flash as the rotating blade snapped the wrench from the mechanic's hand. Indy yanked the mechanic away from the propeller and threw a powerful punch at his opponent's jaw. The mechanic stumbled backwards and struck his head on the side of the plane, collapsing in an unconscious heap below the Flying Wing.

Indy glanced toward the cockpit. The pilot, still adjusting the controls, was oblivious to the fight that had just taken place behind him.

Leaving the mechanic where he was, Indy climbed back up onto the back of the plane. Unfortunately, his intended journey to the cockpit was interrupted once again, this time by menacing laughter from behind. Then a German-accented voice bellowed, "Hey, you now . . . Come here!"

The voice got the attention of the pilot as well as Indy. Both men turned to see the hulking German soldier standing behind the plane. He was now shirtless, and he pumped the air with his massive fists as he waited for Indy to join him on the ground. Like Indy, he was unaware that Marion, at that moment, was removing two wedge-shaped blocks that held one set of the plane's tires in place.

Looking exhausted, Indy slowly climbed down from the back of the plane. It was obvious that the German greatly outweighed him, and the way he held his fists, there was no question that he was an experienced boxer. With those odds against him, Indy knew he wouldn't stand a chance in a fair fight. That's why Indy had no intention of fighting fairly.

He stood before the German and bravely raised his own fists, but then let his gaze drift from his opponent's eyes to something on the ground between them. In fact, Indy wasn't looking at anything in particular, he was just trying to distract the big man. It seemed like a good idea at the time, and as the German followed Indy's gaze, Indy thought it might even work.

While the German was distracted, Indy violated every rule of sportsmanship by kicking his opponent below the belt. Although such a kick would have leveled any ordinary man, the German merely hunched his shoulders at the impact, and fixed Indy with a slightly annoyed look as he waited for Indy to make his next move. With some alarm, Indy thought, *I may as well have kicked a redwood!*

Indy followed with his best punch, but the German ducked it and the punch sailed past him. The German responded with a left jab that caught Indy square on the chin and mouth, knocking him off his feet. Indy landed hard on the seat of his pants, and a moment later, he tasted blood. The German's jab had cut his lower lip.

The German wasn't done with him. The big man urged Indy to get up, and seemed to become infuriated when Indy continued to sit on the ground with a dazed expression on his face. But when the German bent over and grabbed Indy to haul him up to his feet, he suddenly howled in pain as Indy sank his teeth into the man's bare forearm.

The German tossed Indy aside, sending him under the back of the plane. Indy fell against the plane's landing gear, but as the German reached for him, he crouched and ran under the wing, emerging just below the open cockpit. He had assumed that the pilot had remained in his cockpit, but did not expect the pilot to be standing up on his seat with a pistol in his hand. Indy ducked back under the plane as the pilot turned and fired at him. The bullet missed and slammed into the ground.

Unfortunately, the burly German had followed Indy under the plane, and Indy ran straight into the man's fist. The punch sent Indy spinning out from below the Flying Wing, leaving him exposed to the armed pilot. The German moved after him and launched another punch that sent Indy to the ground.

Seeing Indy materialize from beneath the plane, the pilot aimed his pistol at Indy. But before the pilot could fire, the bare-chested German stepped up beside Indy's prone form, blocking the pilot's shot. The pilot raised his pistol's barrel away from his fellow German.

Still on the ground, Indy grabbed a fistful of sand and flung it up into his opponent's face. The German shouted with rage as the sand met his eyes, and then Indy was on his feet again.

As Indy moved away from the big man, the watchful pilot took aim at Indy again. The pilot was about to fire when something struck him from behind and he collapsed into the cockpit. Indy glanced up to see Marion standing on the plane, just behind the cockpit, holding the wedge-shaped blocks that she had removed from the plane's tire. As evidenced by the unconscious pilot, Marion had found a new use for the blocks.

Suddenly, the pilot's body slumped forward onto the controls and throttle. The engines roared louder, revving up, and the plane began to move, rotating around its one still-blocked set of tires. The bare-chested German ignored the roaring engines and punched Indy in the stomach.

Hoping to pull the pilot off the throttle, Marion quickly jumped down into the cockpit. But as she moved, her shoulder bumped into the cockpit's raised canopy, and the canopy slammed down, sealing her inside.

Marion tugged at the pilot's shoulders, but she couldn't budge him. Staring through the canopy's forward window, she saw Indy and the big German, still fighting. She shouted, "Indy!"

The German's fist sank into Indy's stomach again, this time with such force that it lifted Indy off the ground. Gasping for air, Indy wasn't sure how much more he could take. So far, there hadn't been one moment during their fight that the German wasn't practically on top of him, forcing Indy to defend himself with his hands and preventing him from reaching for his whip or gun.

As the plane rotated on the ground, Marion saw a German troop truck drive onto the airfield. Six soldiers rode in the back of the open truck, and when they saw the two men fighting beside the Flying Wing, they reached for their rifles.

Inside the Flying Wing, a small passage led from the cockpit to the glass-domed tail gun. Marion scrambled through the passage, seized the grips on the maneuverable double-barreled machine gun, and took aim at the incoming truck. The soldiers had already begun firing when Marion squeezed the machine gun's triggers. Marion winced at the staccato bursts of gunfire and at the sight of her bullets riddling the truck along with the men on it.

She didn't get them all. One soldier jumped away from the ravaged truck and began firing his own machine gun in Marion's direction as he ran for cover. As the Flying Wing continued its slow rotation on the airfield, Marion felt a mild bump as the starboard wingtip struck the gasoline tanker and knocked a hole in its side. But she kept her attention on the elusive soldier, shooting him down just a moment before he would have moved out of range, and failed to notice the gasoline that was spilling out from the ruptured tanker.

Although Indy heard all the gunfire, he didn't see the wingtip tear through the tanker because the big German was still using him as a punching bag. As Indy went sprawling under the rotating plane, he saw the plane's tires moving toward him and had to roll away fast to avoid getting crushed. As he rolled, his revolver accidentally slid out of its holster and onto the ground. Indy saw the fallen gun and tried to reach for it, but the big German moved in close to the landing gear and Indy instinctively backed away. He nearly stumbled over the still-unconscious mechanic.

Marion thought she had shot all of the soldiers from the truck, but when she spotted another one making a run for it, she swiveled the tail gun after him. The stream of bullets cut down the soldier, but also hit a stack of barrels that were filled with gasoline. As the soldier fell, the barrels exploded with a colossal *boom!* and sent a bright yellow and orange plume of fire into the sky.

The explosion was loud enough to awaken Colonel Dietrich, who had dozed off in his chair outside the command tent. Belloq heard the noise, too, and came running out of the tent to stand beside Dietrich. Both men watched a thick cloud of black smoke rise up from behind a nearby hill, and realized the explosion had come from the airfield.

As Dietrich gaped and rose from his chair, Belloq looked to the crated Ark, which still rested on the ground near Dietrich. Glaring at the soldiers who stood near the crate, Belloq shouted, "Stay with the Ark! Stay with the Ark!"

Dietrich began shouting orders to his men, directing them to the airfield.

Marion was still seated in the domed turret at the Flying Wing's aft when she saw Indy emerge from below the rotating plane and unintentionally move toward one of the spinning propellers. She shouted, "Look out!"

Indy saw the propeller just in time and turned around fast, crouching below the plane as he ran past the landing gear to avoid the big German who pursued him. When Indy came out from under the plane, he looked past the cockpit to see the gas barrels that Marion had shot, which were now blazing away. Then he saw the gas spilling out of the ruptured tanker. The gas was spreading rapidly, flowing across the ground beneath the plane and toward the blazing barrels. As the gas swept under the Flying Wing, the smell was so noxious that it revived the fallen mechanic, who was fortunate to have escaped the path of the plane's tires. With the front of his clothes suddenly soaked in gas, the mechanic began to push himself up, and then ran for safety.

Marion saw the gas and the fire, too. She gasped, "Oh, no!"

"Marion!" Indy muttered.

"In here!" Marion yelled, the enclosed turret muffling her cry. "Up here!"

Moving just below the cockpit, Indy pulled himself up onto the front of the plane and climbed up onto it. As he scrambled over the wing toward the aft, Marion yelled again from inside the turret, "Indy, come on!"

"Hold on!" he shouted back.

"Move up!" she cried as he bent down beside the turret and tried to open it. Watching the gas spread closer to the barrels, Marion cried, "It's gonna blow up!"

Indy was gripping the top of the turret and trying to tug it open when he saw the big German climbing up onto the wing. As the German lunged at him, Indy rolled away from the turret and got up onto his feet. Standing on the wing, he threw his right fist at the German, but the German caught the punch and delivered his own to Indy's jaw. Indy collapsed, slid off the wing, and landed hard on the gas-drenched ground.

"It's stuck!" Marion cried as she fumbled with the turret's opening mechanism. "Indy! I can't push it off!"

Ignoring Marion, the German jumped down after Indy, who remained crumpled beside the plane. The German lifted Indy to his feet, held him at arm's length, and then belted him in the face. Indy reeled but kept his balance, then took another punch to the jaw. The German hit him again, and again.

The gas inched closer to the burning barrels. As bad as Indy hurt, he knew he was Marion's only chance to get out of the Flying Wing. He locked his gaze on the German's nose and threw his right fist into it with everything he had.

There was an ugly crunch as blood suddenly spurted from the German's broken nose, and then Indy launched his left fist at the same target. Indy wasn't aiming at the man's nose so much as he was aiming through it. The German wobbled only slightly on his feet as Indy delivered two more roundhouse punches to his head.

But then the German struck back, slamming his meaty fist into Indy's jaw. Indy saw stars as he toppled to the ground. Rolling onto his side, he looked up at the German, who was now urging him to get up and finish the fight.

The German's eyes were filled with rage, and he kept them fixed on Indy as he pumped the air with his fists. His rage only grew when his opponent looked up at him from the ground and smiled broadly.

Indy kept smiling as he shifted his weight slightly, angling his body so that the German would make another step toward him. Although Indy appeared to be keeping his eyes on the German's face, he was also monitoring the slow rotation of the plane, and the whirring propeller that was closing in behind the big man who stood over him.

Knowing what was about to happen, Indy suddenly flattened himself to the ground and shielded his head with his arms. At first, the big German thought Indy was just trying to distract him again, but then he felt a rush of air against his back. He turned and shouted once before the propeller whipped through him.

Scrambling away from the carnage, Indy found his revolver, snatched it up, and jumped back onto the plane. He looked to the blood-spattered gun turret, saw that it was empty, and thought for a moment that Marion had gotten out. But then, remembering how Marion had moved from the cockpit to the turret, he glanced to the cockpit and saw Marion there, trying her hand at the locking mechanism again.

"It's stuck!" Marion cried.

Carrying his gun in one hand as he ran across the top of the Flying Wing, Indy lowered himself beside the cockpit. He pointed to a crank at the inner edge of the sealed canopy and shouted, "Turn it! Turn it!"

"It's stuck!" Marion repeated.

Pointing to the other end of the crank, he said, "Turn it there!" Before Marion could try, he slapped the canopy window with his hand and snapped, "Never mind! Get back! Get back!"

A split second after Marion threw her body against the far side of the cockpit, Indy fired two bullets directly into the canopy's lock. The lock shattered and Indy threw the canopy open. Just as he reached down to grab Marion's arm and tug her out of the cockpit, the spilled gasoline reached the burning barrels and ignited.

A wave of flame traveled across the airfield as Indy and Marion leaped down from the plane and ran for their lives. They had barely cleared the airfield and were still running side by side when the tanker truck exploded into flames. Barely three seconds later, another explosion rocked the Flying Wing and launched burning debris in all directions.

The debris was still falling when Indy and Marion came to a stop behind a dune. They paused for only a moment to catch their breath. Indy knew the Germans would be swarming all over the airfield within minutes, maybe even sooner.

They had to go back to the camp and find Sallah, and they had to do it fast.

CHAPTER SIXTEEN

By the time the German soldiers and Arab laborers arrived at the airfield, they found nearly every structure and vehicle reduced to smoldering ruins. Smoke still poured from the wreckage of the Flying Wing, and the tanker was nothing but a skeletal frame of black, twisted metal.

"Get the Ark away from this place immediately!" Colonel Dietrich snapped at Gobler as they walked with Belloq past the debris. "Have it put on the truck. We'll fly it out of Cairo." As the three men came to a stop a short distance from the airfield's watchtower, Dietrich glared at his first officer to add, "And Gobler, I want plenty of protection."

Just then, the fires reached some gas barrels that had been carelessly placed near the base of the watchtower. The three men flinched as the barrels exploded and the watchtower burst into flames.

Recovering quickly, Dietrich and Gobler stormed off to direct the soldiers and laborers. Belloq glanced at the burning watchtower, and then surveyed the ruins of everything around him. He didn't have to wonder who was the cause of so much destruction. He *knew*.

"Jones," Belloq muttered harshly.

A few minutes after Dietrich had barked his orders to Gobler, Sallah left the main compound and ran to the airfield. Many laborers had gathered around the ruins of the Flying Wing, and Sallah wanted to see for himself what had happened. But as he ran past a small canvas tent, he was distracted when somebody whistled at him.

Stopping in his tracks, Sallah peered into the tent's dark, triangular opening. He could barely believe his eyes when he saw that Indy and Marion were inside. "Holy smoke, my friends," he said as he ducked to enter the tent and grip Indy's hand while Marion stood in the shadows behind Indy. "I — I'm so pleased you're not dead!"

Then Sallah hunkered down beside Indy and continued, "Indy, Indy, we have no time. If you still want the Ark, it is being loaded onto a truck for Cairo."

"Truck?" Indy said. "What truck?"

Staying out of sight of the soldiers, Indy and Marion stuck close to Sallah as he led them from the tent to a dune that overlooked the compound. When they reached the top of the dune, they kept their heads low and looked to the crated Ark outside the Command Tent, which was surrounded by watchful laborers and soldiers. Two long wooden poles had been secured lengthwise to opposite sides of the crate, and the poles' ends served as handgrips to the four soldiers who picked it up and carried it to the back of a canvas-topped Mercedes troop truck that was parked behind a black open-topped convertible sedan.

The truck's metal tailgate was lowered, and there was an unexpected outcry from the laborers as they saw the soldiers load the Ark onto the truck. From his vantage point, Indy got the impression that the laborers were suddenly eager to prevent the Germans from taking the Ark. A moment after the laborers began shouting and moving toward the truck, a soldier responded by sending a rapid burst of gunfire into the air. Discouraged by the warning shots, the laborers immediately dropped to their knees or sat on the ground, defeated.

As seven soldiers climbed into the back of the troop truck and raised the tailgate, Belloq and Dietrich walked past the truck and got into the back of the convertible. Turning his head back to face the truck's driver, Belloq waved his arm forward and shouted, "Let's go!" A moment later, Toht's black-clad figure slipped into the front passenger seat beside the uniformed driver.

Behind the truck, Gobler strapped on his driving goggles and climbed behind the wheel of a light-armored military car that carried two other men and a turret-mounted machine gun. Behind Gobler's car, a motorcycle with an armed sidecar completed the German convoy.

As the drivers started their vehicles and began to pull away from the compound, Indy glanced at Sallah and Marion and said, "Get back to Cairo. Get us some transport to England — boat, plane, anything. Meet me at Omar's. Be ready for me. I'm going after that truck."

"How?" Sallah asked.

"I don't know," Indy said as he got up to leave. "I'm making this up as I go."

After slipping away from Marion and Sallah, it took Indy less than a minute to find his transport: a magnificent white Arabian stallion that was standing in the shade under a tent. The stallion already had a blanket on its back and leather reins at the ready. Indy climbed on and launched the horse out of the tent. Two Arabs had been sitting on the ground outside, and they jumped up and shouted at Indy as the stallion carried him away.

The stallion was a very different creature than the

type of horse that Indy had learned to ride when he was a boy. So fast and powerful, it seemed less like an animal than a force of nature. Indy held tight to the reins as he guided the stallion across the compound, heading for the road that led past the Command Tent. Beside the large tent, about two-dozen astonished soldiers and the many seated laborers saw Indy's approach. Before the soldiers could even think of taking aim at Indy, their view was blocked by the laborers, who jumped to their feet and shouted as the mounted figure flew past them.

Leaving the compound behind, Indy avoided the dirt road the convoy had taken and went cross-country. He guided the stallion up a steep, rocky hill that brought him to the top of a long ridge. From this point, he had a wide view of the area, allowing him to see not only the rising dust that indicated the convoy's wake but a short-cut that would allow him to catch up with the Germans.

Indy pressed his heels into the horse's sides, and the horse bolted forward along a ridge that traveled parallel to the road. When he looked down to his left, he could see the convoy itself.

Reaching a curve, Indy brought the stallion to a halt. He could see that it was a steep descent to an area where the road below veered off to the left, but he had to trust that his mount could make it. Glancing down at the moving vehicles, Indy's mind raced. He knew that if his timing was right, the horse would carry him down to the road and right behind the canvas-topped truck. Not allowing himself to think what would happen if his timing was off, Indy tightened his grip on the reins and sent the horse down.

Sand and small stones shifted under the stallion's hooves as it managed a skidding run down the slope, but the brave animal followed Indy's commands without fail. When they reached the area where the road curved, the horse ran onto the road directly behind the truck, just as Indy had planned.

The soldiers in the truck shouted in surprise. Their shouts were loud enough that the passengers in the lead vehicle, the convertible, heard them over the noise of the rumbling convoy. From the convertible's rear seat, Belloq looked back over his shoulder.

Because of the way the road twisted through the rocky terrain, Belloq couldn't see anything unusual at first glance, but a moment later Indy and his stallion came into view, trailing alongside the truck. At the sight of his nemesis, Belloq felt a combination of rage and panic.

Directly behind Indy and his stallion, in the military car driven by Gobler, the soldier who manned the gun turret swung his weapon in Indy's direction and opened fire, launching bullets over Gobler's head. The bullets missed Indy, but several pinged off the truck, nearly hitting the soldiers and the crate in the truck's back. The outraged soldiers yelled at the gunner to stop shooting.

The gunner held his fire, allowing Indy to maneuver the galloping stallion up along the truck's right side. When he was close enough to the truck, he leaned out, grabbed at the canvas top, and pulled himself off of the horse's back and onto the side of the truck. The horse whinnied, then began to slow its pace as the truck pulled away with Indy still on it.

As the military car and motorcycle passed the abandoned stallion, Indy quickly shifted his body forward along the truck's side until he stood on the running board that ran below the front passenger door. A soldier sat beside the driver in the truck's front compartment, which was backed by a sheet of solid metal that lacked a rear window. Although the two men had heard the shouts and shots from behind and seen Belloq, Dietrich, and Toht turn their heads in the convertible in front of them, they had neglected to glance at their own rear-view mirrors, and both were unaware that a man had just jumped onto their truck.

In a fluid motion, Indy threw the truck's door open, grabbed the soldier on the passenger side of the long seat, and yanked him out of the truck. The soldier screamed as he tumbled out of the truck and rolled to the side of the road. Then Indy launched himself into the truck and onto the driver. The driver gasped as Indy slammed into him.

Indy wrapped his left arm around the driver's neck as he grabbed at the steering wheel. Wrestling for control of the truck, Indy let his right hand fly from the wheel to the driver's face. The driver snarled as he tried to keep his own grip on the wheel and shove Indy off of him.

Indy elbowed the gearshift as he kicked at the driver's feet and stomped on the brake pedal. He braced himself as the truck abruptly decelerated and let gravity carry the driver's forehead into the dashboard. A moment later, Gobler's car slammed into the back of the truck.

Indy hit the accelerator and the truck lurched forward, causing the crated Ark to slide suddenly toward the back of the truck and into one of the soldiers. The soldier screamed as the crate smashed into his legs and launched him clear over the tailgate. Gobler's car was still directly behind the truck. The falling soldier's head struck and shattered the car's windshield as his body landed hard on the hood.

Indy and the truck driver continued their battle for the wheel as they followed the convertible toward a small

village. The convertible's driver was so distracted by the
swerving truck behind him that he accidentally steered
toward a two-story tall building that was being worked
upon by Arab laborers who stood on rickety wooden
ladders and scaffolding. When Toht saw that they were
headed straight for the construction site, he shouted at
the driver, who swerved to stay on the road.

Unfortunately, when Indy and the truck driver saw
the construction site, they were less than agreeable about
which way to turn. Indy winced as they plowed straight
into the scaffolding and sent the laborers leaping to
safety. One laborer landed on the truck's hood and gaped
for a moment at Indy and the driver through the windshield before he leaped from the truck and rolled to the
ground.

Both Indy and the driver were amazed that they had
made it past the building without killing anyone. Indy
exhaled with relief and grinned at the driver. Despite
their situation and the that fact that they were enemies,
the driver grinned back. The first to remember their
present predicament, Indy's face went grim and he belted
the driver in the jaw.

Indy threw the driver's door open and shoved him
out of the truck, letting him fall down a steep hillside.
Then Indy pulled the door shut and focused on the black

convertible in front of him. He could see Belloq in the back of the car. Belloq looked scared, and Indy couldn't help but feel good about that.

Indy accelerated and rammed the convertible, forcing it off the road. Alongside the road, there was a crude aqueduct, a scrap metal conduit that was elevated by long wooden poles to transport water across the village. The convertible swerved around and under the aqueduct. Indy was keeping his eyes on the convertible, but when it swung out from below the viaduct and shot out at a sharp angle across the road in front of him, he suddenly saw that both the road and the viaduct curved suddenly up ahead.

Indy twisted the steering wheel hard to the side but collided with the wooden poles that supported the viaduct. As the metal conduit broke away and clattered against the truck, it sent water splashing against the windshield.

Regaining control of the truck, Indy followed the convertible away from the village. The road became a series of twisting turns that traveled through a forest of palm trees. Indy glanced to the truck's side-view mirrors to see the car and motorcycle that followed. They were gaining on him.

While the soldiers in the back of the truck watched nervously, Gobler maneuvered his car up along the right side of the truck. At the gun turret behind Gobler, the gunner angled his weapon toward the front of the truck, waiting for the moment he would have a clear shot at Indy.

Indy saw the car coming, and gave the wheel a quick jerk to the right that forced the car off the road. Gobler gnashed his teeth as he steered his car between the trees and over bone-jarring bumps, but managed to get the car back onto the road, a short distance behind the motorcycle.

Thinking the car was no longer a concern, Indy grinned. The grin vanished when he saw the motorcycle and the machine gunner in its sidecar appear in his side-view mirror. But when the motorcycle drew up along the right side of the truck, Indy gave the wheel a jerk to repeat the maneuver that had sent Gobler's off the road. The truck smacked against the sidecar, and the motorcycle spun out and rolled into a deep puddle beside the road. The grin returned to Indy's face.

The motorcyclist and gunner were bruised but otherwise uninjured. As they struggled to their feet beside their ruined vehicle, Gobler's car raced past them.

The forest yielded to a more open, rocky area, and the black convertible raced onward. Indy stayed right behind it, watching Belloq and the outraged Nazis squirm in their seats. Then he saw Gobler's car reappear in his side-view mirror. Annoyed, Indy thought, *Don't these guys know when to quit?*

The car drew up on the left side of the truck. The machine gunner aimed at Indy and began firing. Ignoring the bullets that pinged off the truck's hood, Indy kept his eye on his side-view mirror, waited for the right moment, and then jerked the wheel to the side yet again.

The truck collided against the car, only this time, there weren't any trees to drive into, or anything else for that matter, for the road had brought the vehicles near the edge of a high cliff. Gobler and the two other men screamed as the car plunged from the cliff, carrying them to their deaths.

Indy kept driving after the convertible. As tempted as he was to deal with Belloq and his companions in some harsh fashion, he had not forgotten that his first priority was to deliver the Ark to Sallah in Cairo. He also knew it was only a matter of time before the soldiers in the back of the truck tried something foolish.

He didn't have to wait long.

CHAPTER SEVENTEEN

*I*n the troop compartment behind Indy, the five remaining German soldiers looked at each other anxiously. They could hardly believe that a lone man had managed to overtake their truck and dispose of both Gobler's car and the motorcycle escort. But the soldiers' commanding officer, a tough-looking sergeant, wasn't about to let the American get away with it. Snapping off orders, he instructed four of his men to climb out over the tailgate and make their way up to the front of the truck.

The truck followed the black convertible around a bend, and Indy saw that they were heading through another palm-tree forest. Glancing at his side-view mirrors, Indy saw two soldiers had climbed out onto the left side of the truck, and another two were on the right. Each soldier was hugging the truck's canvas top, clinging to the metal frame below the canvas with one hand as their other hands held their pistols at the ready.

Indy threw the wheel hard to the left. The soldiers tightened their grips on the canvas top as the truck swerved along the edge of the tree-lined road. The overhanging branches and thick leaves of the palm trees whipped at the two soldiers on the left side of the truck, and they screamed as they were knocked from the moving vehicle.

Then Indy swerved to the right, trying to shake off the other two soldiers. They held tight only slightly longer than their left-side comrades, but the combination of Indy's driving and the whipping palm trees was too much for them, too. When Indy heard their cries as they fell from the truck, he smiled with satisfaction.

Indy didn't know that one of the falling soldiers had torn off a large section of canvas from the right side of the truck. The hole in the canvas allowed one of the remaining soldiers to slip out to the side quickly and move up beside the passenger door before Indy could see him coming. Like his predecessors, the soldier clutched a pistol. He landed on the running board and shoved his pistol through the open passenger window.

Indy saw the soldier out of the corner of his eye and moved fast, twisting his body to launch a kick at the passenger door. He wasn't quite fast enough. The soldier fired his pistol and there was a spray of blood as the bullet tore through Indy's leather jacket and hit his shoulder. Indy winced at the sudden pain in his arm, but he still managed a powerful kick that knocked the door open, causing the soldier to swing out and away from the truck.

Gripping the wheel with his left hand, Indy reached for his wounded shoulder with his right. His shoulder hurt like blazes, but he was pretty sure it was just a flesh wound.

The passenger door swung back toward the truck, carrying the soldier with it. The soldier still clutched his pistol, but was using both arms to hang onto the door.

Holding tight to the wheel, Indy shifted his body again to deliver a harder kick to the door and sent the soldier swinging out again. The door's upper hinge snapped off and the entire door bent down and away from the truck.

The soldier clung desperately to the door as his dangling legs dragged against the dirt road. When he glanced up, he saw his sergeant lean out through the hole in the canvas to look at him with a helpless expression.

Indy's vision blurred for a moment, and he blinked his eyes, trying to stay focused on the convertible in front of him. Glancing to his right, he saw the soldier pulling himself back up onto the damaged door. The soldier had his gun out again.

Indy kicked the door for all he was worth. The door bent further out from the truck, and the soldier wailed as he was dragged along the road. Then the door snapped off.

From the troop compartment, the German sergeant saw his last man tumble away with the broken door. Determined to succeed where his men had failed, the sergeant stepped over the tailgate and hauled himself up onto the top of the truck. He kept his body low as he gripped the canvas covering, working his way up toward the front of the truck. Directly above the driver's compartment, there was a tubular metal rack for holding cargo. The sergeant grabbed hold of the bar, and then swung his lower body down through the open window of the driver's door and straight into Indy.

Indy grunted in pain as the sergeant's boots slammed into his injured shoulder and shoved him across the long seat, nearly sending him out through the doorless passenger side. As the sergeant slipped down behind the truck's controls and seized the wheel, he saw Indy clutching at his wounded shoulder in pain. Bracing his knee against the wheel to keep the truck on the road, the sergeant grabbed Indy's arm and began punching his shoulder. Then he seized Indy by the back of his leather jacket and shoved him headfirst into the windshield.

Indy's hat was hardly a protective helmet, but it absorbed some of the impact as he smashed through the windshield and hurtled onto the hood of the moving truck. He bounced on the hot, hard metal and as he slid over the front of the hood, he grabbed at the hood ornament, a circular ring of steel with an inner lambda, the Mercedes logo. The ornament bent and snapped, and Indy fell onto the cargo rack that was set above the bumper in front of the truck's grill.

In the convertible, Dietrich, Belloq, and Toht saw Indy's fall, and they smiled with morbid expectation.

Facing into the truck, Indy clutched desperately at the vertical metal bars on the cargo rack. They bent under his weight, and he threw himself to his right so his stomach landed against the fender of the truck's right front tire. Indy wrapped his arm around the lamp atop the fender and felt the heels of his boots hit and drag against the road. His legs were splayed on either side of the tire. If he lost his grip, he would be flattened.

The sergeant saw the top of Indy's hat above the fender and considered stopping the truck so he could kill the man with his bare hands, but then he noticed Dietrich waving to him from the convertible. Dietrich was gesturing for the sergeant to keep driving, and bring the truck straight up against the convertible's rear bumper. Imagining Indy being crushed between the two vehicles, the sergeant grinned. Then he shifted gears, stomped on the accelerator, and raced toward the convertible.

Realizing what the driver was attempting, Indy shifted his body back in front of the grill, and then lowered himself down from the cargo rack, and past the bumper so that his legs stretched out and dragged under the truck. The rocky ground hammered against the back of his leather jacket as he faced the bottom of the truck and struggled to keep his legs straight. While the truck continued to speed after the convertible, Indy reached up to find a new grip on the undercarriage.

Seeing Indy's action, Dietrich and Belloq waved again at the sergeant, motioning for him to maintain speed by keeping his distance from the convertible.

Indy ignored the pounding that his back was taking and quickly moved hand over hand to reach the truck's rear axle. He nearly lost his grip when he snagged his whip around the axle, but recovered, moving both hands onto the whip. Still clinging to the secured whip's handle, he slid out from under the rear bumper and let out a pained groan as the whip went taut and dragged him after the truck.

Indy rolled onto his stomach and began pulling himself up along the extended whip. He could hardly see what he was doing because of all the sand and dust, but he kept his hat on and stayed focused on the rear bumper as he hauled himself closer to the truck.

When he reached the bumper, Indy pulled his battered body up onto the back of the truck, leaving the whip to trail like an angry snake behind the vehicle. Every movement hurt, but he continued to block out the pain as he scrambled over the tailgate and into the troop compartment. The truck hadn't slowed, and neither did Indy. Moving past the crate that held the Ark of the Covenant, he climbed through the torn canvas and out onto the truck's right side.

Belloq sighted Indy and pointed to the side of the truck as he shouted, "He's there!"

The sergeant looked to his right at the same moment that Indy swung his legs through the space formerly occupied by the passenger door and into the driver's compartment. Indy's boots connected with the stunned sergeant's face, and then Indy shoved the man aside and leaped over him to land behind the wheel. The sergeant looked angry and dazed as Indy grabbed the back of the man's neck. Furious at the way the sergeant had nearly killed him, Indy rammed the sergeant's head into the dashboard before belting him in the jaw. Indy could have shoved the sergeant out through the side of the truck, but in his rage, he gave the man a taste of his own medicine by seizing him with both hands and throwing him out onto the hood.

The sergeant tumbled down past the grille and caught hold of the cargo rack. The bars on the rack bent under his weight, and the sergeant screamed as he fell away and the truck's tires barreled over him.

Indy gnashed his teeth. His entire body felt like a mass of exposed nerves, but he was fueled by his fury at Belloq and the soldiers, as well as by his determination to get the Ark out of Cairo. He stomped on the accelerator and aimed for the black convertible.

The road now stretched past rocky dunes. The convertible's driver tried to veer away from the approaching truck, but Indy swerved hard to the side and forced the convertible off the road. As Belloq's car rolled to a dusty stop, Belloq stood up in the backseat and saw the truck heading off. Turning his gaze to the convertible's driver, he shouted, "Idiot! Idiot!"

The rattled driver put the convertible in reverse and returned to the road. Less than a minute later, Belloq and the Germans were following the truck as it headed to Cairo. But Indy had a good lead on them, and he wasn't about to stop until he reached his destination.

Indy steered the battle-damaged truck through the narrow streets of Cairo until he arrived at Omar's Square, the cul-de-sac where he had arranged his rendezvous with Sallah. There were lots of people in the square, and all of them looked up with excitement as the truck swept past them and headed for the wide-open doors of Omar's Garage. Thanks to Sallah, they were expecting Indy.

Indy guided the truck straight into the garage's shadowy interior, and the moment he brought the truck to a stop, the men outside closed the garage doors, dropped an awning over the doorway, and wheeled a large fruit cart in front of the building.

Mere seconds after Indy had delivered the truck into the garage, the black convertible raced into the square. Because the square was a terminus without any outlets, the driver steered the car into a tight circle before he brought it to a stop. Belloq stood up in the back of the car and surveyed the square. As far as he could see, there were only merchants around, and no sign of Indy.

One young merchant stepped up to the back of the convertible and held out some melons to Dietrich, who had remained seated. He sneered as he snatched a melon from the merchant and hurled it into the road. Fuming and apparently defeated, Belloq sat down beside Dietrich. The convertible took off.

After the black car had left the square, the crowd cheered. They didn't know why Sallah had asked them to conceal Indy and the truck from the Germans, but they had been happy to help Sallah.

Night had fallen and a thick mist had risen over the waterfront when Marion and a very weary Indy walked onto the pier where an old tramp steamer, the *Bantu Wind*, was docked. Indy had his arm wrapped around Marion's shoulder not only out of affection but because he was so sore that he could barely stand, let alone walk.

Sallah walked up to them and grasped Indy's hand. Sallah said, "Everything at last has been arranged."

"The Ark?" Indy said.

"Is on board," Sallah answered. "Nothing is lacking now that you're here." Seeing how stiffly Indy was walking, Sallah added, "Or what is left of you."

A gangplank extended down from the steamer to the pier. Indy glanced at the shifty-looking crew of the *Bantu Wind*, then faced Sallah and asked, "You trust these guys?"

"Yes," Sallah said. He looked to his right to see a lean man standing a short distance away. The man's dark skin contrasted sharply with his white sweater and captain's hat. The man looked away from Sallah as he lit a cigar. Sallah said, "Mr. Katanga."

Simon Katanga was the captain of the *Bantu Wind*. After lighting his cigar, he spat onto the pier before he turned and walked over beside Sallah. Sallah gestured to Indy and Marion, and said, "Mr. Katanga, these are my friends. They are my family. I will hear of it if they are not treated well."

Katanga smiled. "My cabin is theirs," he said graciously. "Mr. Jones, I've heard a lot about you, sir." Surveying Indy's unshaven face and rumpled clothes, he added, "Your appearance is exactly the way I imagined." Katanga glanced at Sallah and both men burst into laughter. Katanga was still chuckling as he headed for the gangplank.

Stepping away from Marion, Indy shuffled over toward Sallah, extended his right hand, and said, "Good-bye."

Ignoring Indy's hand, Sallah threw his arms around Indy and embraced him in a bear hug. Indy grimaced in pain as Sallah said, "Look out for each other. I am already missing you."

Indy pulled gently away from Sallah. Managing a smile, he said, "You're my good friend."

Then Marion stepped up to Sallah and took his hands in hers. "Sallah," she said, and then stood up on her toes to kiss his left cheek. "That is for Fayah . . ." she said, and then she kissed his right cheek and said, "that is for your children, and this is for you." She kissed his mouth, then looked up into his eyes and said, "Thank you."

Sallah was so moved by Marion's words and gesture that he was initially speechless as she and Indy headed for the gangplank, where Katanga stood waiting for them. But a moment later, Sallah burst into song: "*A British tar is a soaring soul, as free as a mountain bird. His energetic fist should be ready to . . . a dictator . . .*"

The other men on the pier smiled and laughed as Sallah, still singing, headed for home.

Indy and Marion boarded the steamer. Indy took comfort in knowing that he had finally recovered the Ark, and that they would soon be on their way to meet his contacts in England. He thought that his worst troubles were behind him.

Unfortunately, he was wrong.

CHAPTER *EIGHTEEN*

*T*he *Bantu Wind* had left Cairo and was on open water under a moonlit sky. Indy was still wearing his hat and dirty clothes as he stretched out on the bunk in Captain Katanga's cabin. He could see the moonlight through the venetian blinds that covered the two portholes that were set above the bunk. Most of the cabin's furniture was built-in, but one eccentricity was a cheval glass, a long mirror mounted on swivels in a frame, which stood near the bed. This particular cheval glass had a mirror on each side of the frame, but Indy didn't need to gaze into either to know he looked awful. He was too tired and worn out to care.

The cabin's door opened and Marion walked in. She had a red blanket wrapped around her upper body and was carrying two metal bowls and some neatly folded white towels.

Indy carefully raised his aching body to sit on the

edge of the bunk. Looking at Marion, he said, "Where did you go?"

"I'm cleaning up," Marion said as she placed the towels and bowls on a wooden table beside the bunk. One of the bowls was filled with water, and the other held washcloths and some small bottles of medicine. She shrugged off the blanket and tossed it onto the bunk beside Indy, revealing that she was wearing a white satin nightgown.

Eyeing the nightgown, Indy said, "Where'd you get *that*?"

"From him."

"Who him?"

"Katanga," Marion said as she soaked a washcloth in water. "I got a feeling I'm not the first woman ever to travel with these pirates."

"It's lovely," Indy muttered.

"Yeah?" Marion said, surprised by Indy's compliment.

"Yeah." Indy winced as he tried to sit up straight.

"Really?" Marion said as she placed the washcloths in a bowl and stepped over to the cheval glass to inspect her reflection in the mirror opposite Indy.

"Yeah," Indy said again, but with more conviction, as he shrugged out of his jacket. He leaned forward and peered into the mirror on his side of the cheval glass.

There was what looked like a slight abrasion on his forehead, just above his left eyebrow. Indy touched the abrasion with the tip of his finger. Despite appearances, it stung fiercely. Indy winced yet again.

Marion couldn't see her reflection clearly because the mirror on her side of the cheval glass was marred by long smudges. She tried wiping a smudge away with her hand, but that only made the smudge worse. Hoping to get a clearer look, and unaware that Indy was leaning close to the glass on the other side, she pushed down on the top of the frame to flip the glass. The action caused the frame's base to swing up and slam hard into the bottom of Indy's chin.

Indy let out a muffled howl.

Peering around the glass to see Indy stroking his injured chin, Marion said, "What'd you say?"

Indy ignored the question and began taking off his shirt. This proved to be something of a challenge. His muscles were so knotted and his fingers were so numb that he couldn't tell what was going on behind his back as he tried to shrug the shirt down past his elbows. Marion left the cheval glass and sat down beside Indy.

"Wait . . ." Indy said as he felt Marion's fingers gently tugging off his shirt. "I don't need any help."

"You know you do," Marion said.

Indy saw his shirtless reflection in the smudged

mirror that now faced him. A strip of white cloth was wrapped around his upper left arm where the bullet had grazed him. Following his pained gaze, Marion said, "You're not the man I knew ten years ago."

"It's not the years, honey, it's the mileage."

Indy shifted his weight and tried to lie down. He still had his hat, pants, and boots on. Seeing that he was having trouble raising his legs up onto the bunk, Marion reached down and lifted his ankles. She said, "You are —"

"Please," Indy interrupted as he lowered his head back against a pillow. "I don't need a nurse. I just want to sleep."

"Don't be such a baby," Marion said. She began cleaning Indy's chest with a damp towel.

"Marion, leave me alone," Indy said as he pushed her hand away.

"What is this here?" she said, touching a bruise on his abdomen.

"Go away," Indy said, and then quickly added, "Yes, it hurts."

Marion moved the damp towel up to Indy's neck. Indy said, "Ow!"

"Well, gosh, Indy," Marion said, flustered, "where *doesn't* it hurt?"

Scowling, Indy pointed to his left elbow and said, "Here."

Unexpectedly, Marion leaned forward and kissed his elbow.

Indy pointed to his forehead, above his right eyebrow. He said, "Here."

Marion removed Indy's hat and tossed it behind her so it landed on the red blanket at the foot of the bunk. Then she leaned down and kissed Indy's forehead.

Marion pulled away. Indy thought for a moment, then reached up to rub the top of his right eyelid. Speaking softly, he said, "This isn't too bad."

Marion kissed his eyelid.

Indy slowly dragged his finger up to the left side of his mouth. As if he weren't entirely certain, he said, "Here?"

Marion kissed Indy's mouth, careful not to press too hard against the split in his lower lip. Indy's head eased back onto the pillow.

Raising herself to look at Indy's face, Marion said, "Jones . . ."

Indy's eyes were closed.

"Jones?!"

Indy was asleep.

Although the crated Ark had been secured in the hold of the *Bantu Wind*, the hold's locked doors did not prevent a visit from some unwelcome passengers: a group of rats that had snuck on board while the steamer had been docked in Cairo.

As the rats scampered past the crate, they became suddenly agitated. They could sense that the crate radiated some kind of danger, something so powerful that it made their whiskers tremble.

The painted swastika on the side of the crate began to burn, sending out blue flames and smoke. A moment later, the flames went out, leaving a charred, black area where the swastika had been.

The nervous rats squeaked and scurried away.

Daylight was sifting through the venetian blinds in the captain's cabin when Marion awakened with a start. It hadn't been the light that caused her to wake up but the sound of Indy loading his gun. She opened her eyes to see Indy standing in the middle of the cabin. He was fully dressed and tucking his gun into his belt.

"What is it?" Marion asked.

"Engines have stopped," Indy said. "I'm going to go check."

Leaving Marion in the cabin, Indy proceeded through a corridor and up a series of metal stairways on the steamer's port side to reach the bridge. On the bridge, he found Katanga, who was returning a corded intercom to its wall mount. Indy said, "What's happening?"

Katanga gestured to the bridge's starboard windows and said gravely, "We have most important friends."

Indy looked out the windows. "Oh, no," he muttered. There was a long, gray submarine in the water, a Nazi U-boat, and a small boat carrying German soldiers advancing on the *Bantu Wind*. Indy picked up a set of binoculars and trained them on the German soldiers who stood atop the sub's conning tower. He didn't recognize any of the soldiers, but it was an easy guess that Belloq and Dietrich were with them.

"I sent my man for you," Katanga said. "You and the girl must disappear. We have a place in the hold. Come on, go, go, go."

Indy wore a stunned expression as he lowered the binoculars.

"Come on," Katanga urged, "go, my friend, go."

Moving fast, Indy left the bridge. But just as he rounded a corner to descend a flight of stairs, he saw another boatload of soldiers had already boarded the *Bantu Wind*. The soldiers were brandishing rifles and machine guns, and Indy realized he'd have to try a different route back to the captain's cabin or risk being sighted by the soldiers. Indy slunk off into another corridor, hoping that he could make it back to Marion before the Germans found her.

The soldiers began searching every room and chamber. They threw open a hatch to find a hold full of pirates who raised their hands in surrender. None of the pirates revealed any information about Indy or Marion, so the soldiers kept looking.

Indy pulled his gun from his belt as he arrived at the end of the corridor that led to the captain's cabin. Running quickly but quietly, he was but a few strides from the cabin's door when he heard a man's German accented voice from within. "Where is Dr. Jones?" the man demanded.

"What's the big idea?" Marion answered. "Let go!"

Indy's mind raced. Knowing he wouldn't be any use to Marion if he were captured, too, he ducked into an empty vestibule to conceal himself. A split second later, a German soldier shoved Marion out of the cabin, and she struck the corridor wall hard with her shoulder.

Marion was still wearing her white nightgown. She leaned against the wall as three German soldiers stepped out of the cabin and into the corridor. Each soldier gripped a machine gun. Marion glared at the soldier who'd shoved her and jabbed his chest with her finger as she said, "Don't you touch me."

The soldier grabbed Marion by her upper arm and escorted her out of the corridor.

Indy heard Marion and the soldiers walk past his hiding place. Knowing that the soldiers would come back looking for him, he tried to think of a better place to hide. He found a hatch that led to a tubular ventilation shaft and climbed up into it.

Indy saw light at the top of the shaft, and poked his head up to peer out through an air-scoop ventilator. The ventilator was positioned beside the abaft funnels that vented gases from the steamer's boiler. A German soldier stood near the ventilator, facing away from Indy's position to survey the deck, where other soldiers were herding the *Bantu Wind*'s subdued crew out into the open.

A winch was suspended over the open hatch of the main hold, and Indy saw the Germans hoisting the crated Ark up through the hatch. And then he saw Marion, who was bracketed by a pair of soldiers.

Stepping onto the deck, Marion saw Dietrich and Belloq standing among the soldiers who had apprehended the crew. As Dietrich turned slowly to face her, Marion felt her rage boil over at the sight of the man who'd shoved her into the Well of Souls. Marion stepped boldly away from her escorts and raised her hand to punch Dietrich.

Katanga saw Marion's approach and he reached out fast to catch her wrist, and then pulled her away from Dietrich and held her in front of him protectively. Seeing the fire in Marion's eyes and how their captain had stopped her from striking Dietrich, Katanga's crew burst into laughter. Even Belloq found himself chuckling.

Dietrich lifted his angry gaze to four soldiers who stood above the deck on the bridge and shouted, "What about Jones?!"

"There's no trace yet, sir!" one soldier answered.

"Jones is dead," Katanga said.

Surprised by Katanga's claim, Dietrich turned to face Katanga, who still held Marion in front of him. Katanga continued, "I killed him. He was no use to us."

From inside the air-scoop ventilator, Indy heard Katanga's words. The soldier who stood near the ventilator lit a cigarette, and Indy winced as the smoke drifted back into his face.

"This girl, however," Katanga continued, "has certain value where we're headed. She'll bring a very good price." Katanga stroked Marion's hair and lifted it as if he were inspecting something of exceptionally fine quality. Smiling at Dietrich, Katanga said, "Mmm? Herr Colonel, that cargo you've taken ..." Katanga tilted his chin to the crated ark. "If it's your goal, go in peace with it, but leave us the girl. It would reduce our loss on this trip."

"Savage!" Dietrich snarled at Katanga, who made no response to the Nazi's insult. "You are not in the position to ask for anything," Dietrich continued. "We will take what we wish." Grabbing Marion by her upper arm, he added, "And then decide whether or not to blow your ship from the water." Dietrich pulled Marion away from Katanga.

Indy ducked fast as the nearby soldier turned and tossed his cigarette butt into the ventilator. Indy felt the still-burning butt land on his shoulder and he wriggled silently to snatch it up and extinguish it before lowering himself out of the vent.

As Dietrich escorted Marion from the deck, Belloq stopped them and said, "The girl goes with me." Facing Dietrich, he continued, "She'll be part of my compensation. I'm sure your Führer would approve." Belloq turned his attention to Marion. As he removed his jacket and draped it over Marion's shoulders, he said, "If she fails to please me, you may do with her as you wish. I will waste no more time with her now." Then he faced Dietrich again and said dismissively, "Excuse me." Belloq wrapped his arm around Marion and guided her away from Dietrich.

After the Germans and Belloq left with Marion and the crated Ark for the waiting submarine, Katanga stood at the rail on the *Bantu Wind* and faced the sub. A crewman moved up beside Katanga and said, "I can't find Mr. Jones, captain. I've looked everywhere."

"He's got to be here somewhere," Katanga said, letting his gaze drift from the sub to his steamer's bridge. "Look again."

A moment later, the crewman said, "I found him."

"Where?"

The crewman pointed to the sub and said excitedly, "There!"

Katanga followed the crewman's gaze to see Indy swimming beside the German sub. The sub's engines had just started when Indy grabbed hold of its hull and pulled his dripping body onto the deck.

In his haste to reach the sub, Indy had left his hat, jacket, and other gear on the *Bantu Wind*, but managed to tuck his whip into his safari shirt. As he caught his breath and pushed himself up from the sub's deck, he heard the steamer's crew cheering for him across the open water. He waved to the crew, and then ran quickly toward the sub's conning tower and climbed up onto it.

What now? Indy wondered. The sub's upper hatch was sealed from the inside, and he wasn't about to knock and let the Germans know he was still alive and had hitched a ride. Indy had no idea where the sub might be headed, but if it completely submerged, he'd be in deep trouble. As resilient as he was, he could only hold his breath for so long.

The submarine moved away from the *Bantu Wind*, carrying Indy with it.

CHAPTER NINETEEN

*T*he German U-boat was named *Wurrfler*, and Indiana Jones was fortunate that the sub's periscope remained above the water's surface as it traveled across the Mediterranean Sea. He was even more fortunate that he'd brought his whip, for he used it to tie himself to the periscope, and relieve his aching arms and hands from the task of hanging on as the sub sped to its destination. Still, by the time the sub began its approach to an island north of Crete, Indy was cold, tired, and soaked to the bone.

The sub's conning tower lifted from the water as the sub steered toward the base of a high, rocky cliff. As Indy untied himself from the periscope and recoiled his whip, he saw what at first appeared to be a cave at the cliff's waterline, but then he saw lights inside the cave, and realized it was a submarine pen. Indy knew there were probably some German lookouts stationed at the mouth of the pen, so he moved cautiously down from the sub's conning tower, and then eased himself off the deck and into the cold water. He clung to the side of the sub, letting it carry him toward the pen.

He heard a clang from above, and realized some members of the sub's crew had opened the upper hatch and were stepping onto the deck. Indy kept his head low, and then released his grip on the sub. He stealthily swam after the sub and into the pen.

The sub pen was a long, narrow chamber with high stone walls that were decorated with Nazi banners and flags. Two elevated platforms ran the length of the pen on either side of the man-made canal that allowed the U-boat to float in. Indy spotted a ladder that traveled up from the waterline to the platform on his right. He seized the bottom rung of the ladder and began to haul himself up.

Keeping to the shadows, Indy snuck past a group of German soldiers who stood on the platform, watching the sub's arrival. The sub was still floating to a stop when Indy found a convenient hiding place behind some tarpaulin-covered ordnance.

Indy wanted to get closer to Marion and the Ark. To accomplish that, he realized he needed to disguise himself in a German uniform. He ducked down behind the tarp as three soldiers walked toward his position. While two of the soldiers continued walking, one came to a stop and turned his back to Indy so he could face the sub.

Two soldiers were visible on the sub's conning tower, and more soldiers were standing on the opposite platform. All of them had a clear view of the tarp that shielded Indy, but they were focusing on the sub. Indy tried not to think about them. He didn't want to miss what might be his best or only chance to get a uniform. He took a couple of deep breaths, and then leaned out from his hiding spot.

Indy grabbed the nearby soldier by the back of his jacket, and yanked him off his feet and over the tarp. The soldier was so startled that no sound left his mouth as Indy slammed him to the platform floor. Indy belted the soldier and knocked him out cold.

Raising his gaze from the unconscious soldier, Indy peeked out from his position to see Marion emerge on the deck of the sub. Her escort was a soldier who had his machine gun leveled at her. Indy saw that the soldier's head was bandaged and his left arm was in a sling. Belloq and the Nazi in the black hat and leather trench coat — Indy didn't know his name — followed Marion and the wounded soldier onto the deck. Indy hoped that Marion was responsible for the soldier's injuries, but for all he knew, the soldier may have been one of the guys that he'd shaken off the troop truck during the trip from Tanis to Cairo. In their olive drab and khaki uniforms, the German soldiers had started to look alike to Indy.

But less than a minute later, he learned that the soldiers were definitely not all alike, or at least that they came in different sizes. He had removed the unconscious soldier's uniform shirt as well as his own safari shirt, but as he sat with his back to the tarp and tried to pull on the soldier's jacket, he realized he was unable to button it. It was simply too small for him. He thought, *Of all the rotten luck!*

While Indy turned his head to see if any other soldiers might be standing nearby, he heard a voice speaking from almost directly above him. Still seated, Indy turned and looked up at another soldier who had walked up to him from out of nowhere, and who now loomed over him, speaking in rapid German.

Wearing an embarrassed, sheepish smile, Indy rose from the platform and stood before the soldier. Indy didn't understand German very well, but could tell that the soldier was reprimanding him for his unkempt appearance. Indy pulled a comb from his pocket and dragged it through his hair while the soldier prattled on with additional criticisms and reached out to adjust the collar of Indy's ill-fitting stolen jacket. Indy was no expert on German soldiers, but he knew two things about this one in particular. First, he was a fool. Second, he was about the same size as Indy.

Indy brought his knee up fast into the soldier's abdomen. The soldier doubled over, and Indy used his other knee to clip the soldier's jaw. The soldier's cap sailed up in front of Indy, who caught it as the soldier collapsed at his feet.

Indy put the cap on his head. It fit just right. So did the rest of the soldier's clothes.

While Indy changed, the crated Ark was hoisted out from the U-boat and placed on the deck near Belloq. As Dietrich walked past Toht and the captive Marion to arrive beside the Frenchman, a soldier stepped out onto the opposite elevated platform, gazed down at Belloq, and said, "The altar has been prepared in accordance with your radio instructions, sir."

"Good," Belloq replied. "Take the Ark there immediately."

The soldier nodded and walked off.

Belloq stepped over to the crated Ark and looked at the crate's scorched surface. He didn't think there was anything unusual about the way the German lettering and Nazi emblem had been burned away. He assumed that either Indiana Jones or the crew of the *Bantu Wind* was responsible, that they had just been trying to erase evidence that they had taken the crate from the Nazis. He checked the ropes that wrapped around the crate to make sure they were secure.

Stepping close to Belloq, Dietrich said, "Monsieur . . . I am uncomfortable with the thought of this . . . Jewish ritual." The racist Dietrich said *Jewish* with obvious distaste. "Are you sure it's necessary?"

Belloq pursed his lips in mild irritation. He had explained to Dietrich that opening the Ark required the recitation of Hebrew prayers, and that he would wear elaborate ceremonial robes for the occasion. As the winch began to lift the crated Ark from the sub's deck, Belloq replied, "Let me ask you this: Would you be more comfortable opening the Ark in Berlin, for your Führer? Finding out, only then, if the sacred pieces of the Covenant are inside? Knowing, only then, whether you have accomplished your mission, and obtained the one true Ark?"

Not surprisingly, Dietrich offered no response. He didn't even want to think of what might happen to him if he failed his mission.

Belloq walked up a gangplank and onto the elevated platform that bordered the port side of the docked U-boat. As he walked past a stack of oil barrels, his shoulder connected hard with a German soldier who walked from the opposite direction. The soldier did not stop to apologize to Belloq but averted his gaze as he kept walking toward the barrels. Belloq wondered if the soldier had deliberately bumped into him, but because he had more important things on his mind, he moved on.

Standing beside the oil barrels, the disguised Indy glanced at Belloq's departing form. There had been no smart reason to bump into Belloq, but Indy had just felt like it. When the time was right, he hoped he'd have the opportunity to bump Belloq right off the planet.

Indy looked up to see an automated winch carry the crated Ark across the sub pen. Indy had overheard the soldier tell Belloq that an altar had been prepared for the Ark. He had no plan for saving Marion or getting them both off the island, but he knew he had to do whatever he could to make sure that the Ark never reached that altar.

Belloq and Dietrich led a procession that included Marion, Toht, and two-dozen German soldiers through a steep, sandy canyon that traveled away from the secret U-boat pen. Marion, still wearing the white gown that Katanga had given her, was followed by Nazi flag bearers. Behind them, four soldiers carried the Ark of the Covenant, which had been removed from its scorched crate and was now draped under a dark blue sheet to protect it from the harsh sunlight. Toht removed his black hat and used a handkerchief to mop the top of his sweaty head.

At the very rear of the procession was Indy, who walked quietly and tried not to draw any attention. Although his stolen uniform fit well enough, his unshaved face was definitely not in keeping with the other soldiers. He had been unable to obtain any weapons when he left the sub pen, so when the procession flowed past tall stacks of crates that contained military supplies, he fell back and then darted between the crates.

Indy had hoped to get his hands on a machine gun, but in the first crate he opened, he found something even more devastating, and also astonishing. It consisted of a long metal tube with an explosive warhead attached to the end of it; from an illustration on the inside of the crate, Indy realized that it was an anti-tank weapon, an expendable preloaded grenade launcher. Remembering the Flying Wing back at the Tanis site, Indy wondered, *What will the Nazis think up next?!*

Indy slung the grenade launcher over his shoulder and then scrambled up a steep slope. When he reached the top of the ridge, he kept moving until he arrived at the top of a cliff that overlooked the canyon. Seconds later, Belloq, Dietrich, and Marion came into view along with the rest of the procession. From above, the Nazi in the leather trench coat looked like a moving black blot against the sand.

"Hello!" Indy shouted.

The startled soldiers stopped and turned, raising their guns. The soldiers who had been carrying the Ark gently placed it on the ground so they could draw their own weapons. Marion, Belloq, Dietrich, and Toht turned and looked up, too. They all saw Indy on the cliff, aiming the grenade launcher at the Ark.

Belloq and Dietrich gaped. Marion beamed.

"Jones?" Belloq gasped. Then he stepped forward and shouted, "Jones!"

Indy answered, "I'm going to blow up the Ark, René!"

The sight of Indiana Jones made Toht feel queasy. He shuffled away from the soldiers and sat down on a low rocky ledge.

Marion bolted away from Belloq and Dietrich, but was immediately seized by two soldiers who held her fast near the ledge where Toht sat.

"Your persistence surprises even me," Belloq said to Indy. Then he muttered, "You're going to give mercenaries a bad name."

"Dr. Jones," Dietrich said, stepping forward. "Surely you don't think you can escape from this island?"

"That depends on how reasonable we're all willing to be!" Indy answered, keeping the grenade launcher trained on the Ark. "All I want is the girl!"

Still in the clutches of the two soldiers, Marion beamed more brightly.

Dietrich glanced at Belloq, who was using his hat to fan his face. Belloq shook his head. Returning his gaze to Indy, Dietrich said, "If we refuse?"

"Then your Führer has no prize."

Belloq looked to the soldiers who stood around the Ark and said, "Okay, stand back." He shook his hat at them, motioning them to move aside. "All of you, stand back. Get back."

The soldiers obeyed. Then Belloq placed his hat on his head, walked over to stand beside the Ark, and said, "Okay, Jones. You win. Blow it up."

Shocked by Belloq's words, Dietrich mumbled a command under his breath. The troops responded by moving toward the Ark to defend it, but then Belloq snatched a machine gun from a soldier and leveled its barrel at the others. The soldiers looked at him uncer-

tainly, but something in Belloq's eyes convinced them
that he was the one in control of the situation.

Tearing his gaze from the soldiers, Belloq glared at
Indy and shouted, "Yes, blow it up! Blow it back to God.
All your life has been spent in pursuit of archaeological
relics. Inside the Ark are treasures beyond your wildest
aspirations." Belloq smiled. "You want to see it open as
well as I," he continued as he lowered the machine gun.
"Indiana, we are simply passing through history. This . . ."
He gestured to the Ark. "This *is* history."

All eyes were on Indy, wondering whether he would
pull the grenade launcher's trigger.

Belloq said, "Do as you will."

Indy felt his stomach churn. He hadn't been
operating with much of a plan, just trying to stay alive
and keep one step ahead of the bad guys as usual. But he
hadn't expected Belloq to call his bluff either. He felt
disgusted that Belloq knew him well enough to know
that he never had any intention of destroying the Ark,
and felt even worse because he had failed Marion.

Utterly defeated, Indy lowered the grenade launcher.

Four soldiers had worked their way up to Indy's position. They moved in behind him, their machine guns
aimed at his back. When they took the grenade launcher
from him, he didn't offer any resistance.

CHAPTER TWENTY

*N*ight had fallen by the time the Nazis had finished preparing their makeshift altar for the Ark of the Covenant and Belloq's ritual. The site was a remote area of the island, where wide, staggered stones served as a stairway up to a natural amphitheater, an open space surrounded by high, rocky walls. The soldiers had set up a portable generator to power a series of klieg lights that were positioned around the altar, and also a motion picture camera to record the ritual for prosperity.

Indy and Marion were tied back-to-back to a tall lamp pole that jutted up from the ground at the outer edge of the amphitheater. They craned their necks and watched as two soldiers removed the blue sheet from the Ark and then lifted the Ark up the stone steps to the altar, where Belloq, Dietrich, and Toht awaited. The soldiers set the Ark down in front of Belloq, and then stepped back.

Belloq wore a turban and ceremonial robes with a jeweled breastplate, and held an ornate staff that was decorated with a sculpted ram's head. Indy thought Belloq looked ridiculous. Blasphemous, too.

In a low, solemn tone, Belloq began reciting a Hebrew prayer. When he was done, he gestured to the two soldiers who had remained standing on either side of the Ark. The soldiers moved toward the Ark and slowly removed its lid.

Dietrich and Toht moved up on either side of Belloq to peer inside. The anxious soldiers who stood below their position took a few cautious steps forward, hoping that they, too, might be able to see the Ark's contents.

It was Dietrich who leaned down to reach into the Ark. When he lifted his hand, he was holding nothing but sand, which was all that remained of the sacred Ten Commandments.

As the sand filtered through Dietrich's fingers, a stunned looking Belloq lunged forward to catch the sand in his own hand. Dietrich sneered as he threw the sand down in disgust and turned away from the Ark. The realization that the Ark contained nothing but sand prompted Toht's face to crease into a sick smile, and then he began to laugh. Toht turned away from the Ark, too, leaving Belloq clutching at sand.

Indy grinned. He hadn't imagined the possibility that

the Ten Commandments had been long reduced to dust. Belloq may have obtained the Ark, but it appeared that history itself had stopped him from trying to use its contents for some supernatural purpose. Not that Indy believed in that sort of thing.

Suddenly, there was a strange vibration and a whirring sound in the air, and bright blue-white sparks began flying from the power generator. One by one, the klieg lights started exploding, spraying bits of glass at the surprised soldiers. The generator flung more sparks, some of which struck the soldiers' rifles. The soldiers reflexively dropped the hot metal to the ground.

Indy felt the wind begin to pick up.

A low, growling sound seemed to emanate from the open Ark. Clutching the ram's head staff, Belloq peered into the Ark again. A light appeared to glow from deep within the Ark's dark interior, so deep that Belloq wondered if the Ark had somehow opened an access to an ancient well, or some more mysterious place.

A strange, luminescent white mist rose up from inside the Ark and spilled out over the altar. The mist began flowing down the stone steps, moving over the soldiers and the surrounding rocks, past Marion and Indy.

Indy wasn't sure what was happening, or what was about to happen, and that made him nervous. Despite his repeated claims that he wasn't superstitious, something inside him told him that an unknown force *had* been unleashed.

Indy's mind raced as he strained at the ropes that bound him and Marion to the lamp pole. *What if the stories about Tanis weren't just myths?* he thought, casting his mind back to his meeting with Brody and the Army officials. What was it Brody had said about the lost city? "Wiped clean by the wrath of God" — just like Sodom and Gomorrah. Thinking of Lot's wife, who had been turned to a pillar of salt when she looked upon God's destruction of Sodom, Indy turned his head away from the Ark and the soldiers and tried to relax his body against the pole as he spoke in a voice so low that only Marion could hear: "Marion, don't look at it. Shut your eyes, Marion. Don't look at it, no matter what happens."

Marion looked up at the sky, where dark, ominous clouds had suddenly appeared. Then she closed her eyes.

The mist continued to pour out of the Ark. To the amazement of Belloq, Dietrich, Toht, and the watchful soldiers, long wisps of light appeared to extend from the mist, and then transformed into unearthly apparitions. Some of the apparitions resembled cloaked, ghostlike beings. The apparitions flew rapidly through the air, circling the soldiers.

Some soldiers just stood speechless as they watched the apparitions and ducked away from them. Others twisted uncomfortably as the apparitions passed through their bodies. When one apparition whipped past Toht, the Nazi regarded it with an openly bemused expression.

Belloq gazed at a cloaked apparition that flew before him and sighed. A moment later, the apparition lifted its head to reveal what appeared to be a lovely, female face.

"It's beautiful!" Belloq cried out in wonderment.

The apparition turned and lifted its head to Toht. Toht's lips twitched as he eyed the apparition skeptically through his glasses. And then, unexpectedly, the apparition's face transformed into a sneering death's head.

Toht screamed.

Indy heard the scream. So did Marion. As the wind and mist whipped about them, Marion shouted, "Indy?!"

"Don't look, Marion!" Indy repeated. "Keep your eyes shut!"

Belloq's eyes went wide as he returned his gaze to the nether regions of the Ark's interior. A bright light shimmered up from within the Ark and swept over Belloq's head and torso. Then his eyes blazed, and twin bolts of bright energy streaked out from his eyes and into the soldiers. The soldiers jerked as the bolts struck and then passed through them, tearing out from their backs and into the neighboring soldiers. It happened so fast that none of the soldiers had time to scream, let alone make any effort to flee. One blast of energy tore straight through the motion picture camera — destroying the film within — and the head of the soldier who had been operating it. The rippling energy radiated from Belloq's eyes until each soldier was struck. The soldiers' knees buckled, and they collapsed to the ground.

But the light from within the Ark wasn't through with Belloq. As his head blazed with energy, Dietrich's eyes went wide and a horrified moan escaped from his gaping mouth, and Toht shrieked louder. Belloq screamed as he raised his hands to the sides of his head. Then Dietrich and Toht began to literally melt, screaming in agony as the intensity of the blazing energy boiled the flesh off their skeletons.

Belloq howled, and then his entire body exploded.

Moving like a massive wave, a wall of flame and smoke surged away from the altar, crashing over the dead soldiers and cremating them instantly. Still tied to the pole, Indy and Marion felt the heat rush past them, but kept their eyes shut as they screamed and braced themselves for death.

And then, the wave of flame surged back toward the altar, as if the Ark were now inhaling the destruction it had just exhaled. Then the Ark sent a column of fire straight up into the night sky, so powerful that it launched the Ark's lid spinning into the air and created a hole in the clouds that hung over the island.

The fire carried the Ark's lid high up beyond the clouds, but then the fire arced back toward Earth. The Ark's lid came down, too, and landed back in its place atop the Ark with a resounding thud, which was followed by a distant, thunderous boom.

Indy listened to the thunder, and sensed that the danger had passed. He opened his eyes tentatively, and then turned his head to look down at his right arm. With some surprise, he lifted his wrist to see the smoldering remains of the rope that had bound him to the pole.

Brushing the rope from his wrist, he reached around to touch Marion's shoulders, turned her to face him and said, "Marion."

Marion's eyes were still closed, and she was trembling. A moment later, she cautiously opened her eyes, and then threw herself into Indy's arms. Neither one of them was entirely certain of what they had survived, but both were glad to be alive.

When they ended their embrace, they looked to the altar. There wasn't any sign of Belloq or the Germans, but the Ark of the Covenant rested exactly where the soldiers had placed it.

Indy remembered seeing some radio equipment among the stacks of military supplies outside the sub pen. He hoped some of that equipment still worked, or it was going to be a long swim home.

CHAPTER TWENTY-ONE

Shortly after returning to the United States with Marion and the Ark of the Covenant, Indiana Jones — clean shaven and wearing a decent suit — and Marcus Brody were sitting around a conference table with the two men from U.S. Army Intelligence, Colonel Musgrove and Major Eaton, in a large oak-paneled room in the War Office building in Washington, D.C. A fifth man, a rotund fellow who wore a cheap sportcoat, thick rimmed glasses, and a humorless expression, listened silently to the others as he leaned against a nearby file cabinet. Musgrove and Eaton hadn't introduced the man, but the way the conversation had been going, Indy and Brody hadn't seen any point in asking who he was.

"You've done your country a great service," Musgrove said to Indy.

Puffing at his pipe, Eaton added, "And we, uh, trust you found the settlement satisfactory."

"Oh, the money's fine," Indy said, trying to remain calm. "The situation's totally unacceptable." He couldn't believe Musgrove and Eaton had lied to him and Brody. They'd *never* planned on allowing the Marshall College Museum to keep the Ark of the Covenant.

Ignoring Indy's comment, Eaton said, "Well, gentlemen, I guess that just about wraps it up."

In a measured tone, Brody said, "Where is the Ark?"

"I thought we'd settled that," Eaton said petulantly. "The Ark is somewhere very safe."

"From *whom*?" Indy said.

As Eaton tossed an irritated glance at Indy, Brody said, "The Ark is a source of unspeakable power, and it has to be researched."

"And it *will* be, I *assure* you, Dr. Brody," Eaton said in his most placating tone, then turned to Indy and added, "Dr. Jones. We have top men working on it right now."

Indy leaned forward in his chair, stared hard at Eaton, and said, "*Who*?"

Eaton held Indy's gaze and repeated slowly, "Top . . . men."

After his meeting with Musgrove and Eaton, Indy could hardly wait to leave the War Office building. Marion had been waiting for him at the top of the grand stairway in the lobby, but he brushed past her as he put on his hat and started down the steps, heading for the exit.

"Hey, what happened?" Marion said as she ran down the steps to catch up. "You don't look very happy."

"Fools," Indy muttered. "Bureaucratic fools."

"What'd they say?"

Stopping on the steps, Indy turned to face Marion. "They don't know what they've got there," he fumed.

Smiling at Indy, Marion said, "Well, I know what I've got here. Come on. I'll buy you dinner."

Indy looked down at his shoes. Marion reached up to lift the brim of his hat.

Indy looked at Marion. She was wearing a pale tan jacket with a matching skirt and a broad-brimmed hat. She really was lovely.

Indy turned away from Marion, but then stuck his left elbow out. Marion linked her arm around his, and then they proceeded down the steps. As Indy wondered about the fate of the Ark, he cast one last glance over his shoulder before they left the building. This adventure may have been over, but a new one would surely be coming.

The Ark of the Covenant wound up in a new wooden crate, custom built for its dimensions. After the crate's lid was lowered and nails sealed it shut, a stencil was slapped on the side of the crate so that black paint could indicate:

TOP SECRET
ARMY INTEL. 9906753
DO NOT OPEN!

The last "top man" to see the Ark was a little old man who worked in a warehouse in a government building. After he nailed the crate shut, he loaded it onto a metal hand truck and pushed it down an aisle that was lined by stacks of similarly marked crates. It was a long aisle because there were a lot of crates, some stacked five or six high. How many crates were there? More than the old man had ever cared to count.

In fact, after all his years of government employment, he really had no idea how many crates were stored in the warehouse. He didn't even know anything about the contents of the crates. He was only paid to put things into storage, not remember what was in them, and that was good enough for him. But if he had to guess, he would have estimated there were thousands of crates in the warehouse.

Maybe more.